P9-DCC-829

Nibbles

AND THE
CRAZY SCIENCE
EXPERIMENT

BARBARA STAVETSKI

NIBBLES AND THE
CRAZY SCIENCE EXPERIMENT

TP THE TOWNSEND LIBRARY

For more titles in the Townsend Library,
visit our website: **www.townsendpress.com**

Copyright © 2014 by Townsend Press, Inc.
Printed in the United States of America

9 8 7 6 5 4 3 2 1

Illustrations © 2014 by Hal Taylor

All rights reserved. Any **one** chapter
of this book may be reproduced without
the written permission of the publisher.
For permission to reproduce more than
one chapter, send requests to:

Townsend Press, Inc.
439 Kelley Drive
West Berlin, NJ 08091
permissions@townsendpress.com

ISBN-13: 978-1-59194-433-1
ISBN-10: 1-59194-433-3

Library of Congress Control Number:
2013955164

CONTENTS

My Name Is Buzzy Baxter 1

1. The Science Experiment 3

2. Mixing Up the Chemicals 9

3. The Bubble Blast 15

4. Nibbles 21

5. The Hamster Can Talk 26

6. The Gigantic Socks 36

7. Sneaking into School 48

8. The Hamster-Napping Plot 56

9. The Hulk 63

10. Good Grub 74

11. Nibbles Gets Lost 86

12. Pet Corral 98

13. Yummy Yummy Churros 106

14. Get Me Out! 111

15. The Stubborn Hamster 122

16. Return of the Hulk 130

17. Candy Corn Math 141

18. Disaster Strikes 153

19. The Sound of Silence 159

20. Into the Sunset 166

MY NAME IS BUZZY BAXTER

. . . and I have a story to tell about a fourth grade science experiment that led to a crazy result.

My full name is Bertram Aloysius Baxter. Dorky, right? Lucky for me, back in second grade, my best friend Jeff Woodhouse nicknamed me Buzzy, and the name stuck. I was born on April Fool's Day—my parents say that's why I'm such a joker. I have a little sister named Max and a baby brother on the way. Or maybe another sister, as Mom and Dad keep reminding me. Also living in our house is my grandma from California, who we call Grams. She's staying until the baby comes.

I'm in fourth grade at Filbert Elementary School in Mr. Del Duca's class. I have the best seat in the room, back by the table that holds the hamster cage.

Mr. Del Duca—Mr. D, for short—brought the hamster to class the first week of school. We named the little guy Nibbles because of the way he nib-nib-nibbles with his tiny hamster teeth. Nibbles has shiny brown eyes and fur the color of Goldfish crackers. He likes eating Goldfish crackers too, and I sneak him a few now and then. Hamsters usually sleep during the day and play at night, but the noise in our classroom keeps Nibbles awake a lot during school time.

Okay—you've met me and you've heard about Nibbles. Time to start the story . . .

CHAPTER
1

THE SCIENCE EXPERIMENT

Mr. Del Duca is the first man teacher I've ever had. He played basketball in college, and he keeps telling us that he turned down a thirty-million-dollar pro contract to become a teacher and mold impressionable young minds. I tell him he should have taken the thirty-mil and let someone else do the molding. But Mr. D has us do some pretty sweet stuff in school. Like the science experiments. That's why we like him.

"This year in science class, you're going to learn about the scientific method," he told us the first week of school. "And"—Mr. D shot us a wink—"you'll have fun doing it. Here's the plan. Every week you'll perform an experiment, the way scientists work in their labs. Before the experiment, you'll predict what you think will happen. Afterward, you'll draw conclusions."

The first experiment involved a hair dryer and a ping pong ball. Mr. D tossed the little white ball from hand to hand. "You all know what happens if I drop this ball?"

"Gravity grabs it," I hollered out. "And it hits the floor. Like this!" I flung myself sideways and toppled onto the floor. That brought laughs from the class.

Mr. D didn't look amused. "Thanks for reminding us how gravity works, Buzzy. Now, back at your desk and listen up. So . . . we all know how gravity works. But what do you think will happen if I turn on the hair dryer, aim the air flow at the ceiling, and drop the ball over the hair dryer?"

"The air will send the ball flying across the room," said Super Matt.

"You oughta know," I put in quickly. "Super Matt's an expert on flying, right?" That got another laugh from kids. Only Mr. D and Cari, the new girl across the aisle from me, looked puzzled. They didn't know we'd starting calling Matt Kelly "Super Matt" back in kindergarten, when he wore his Superman cape to school every single day.

"Okay, that's our prediction." On the board Mr. D wrote *BALL WILL FLY ACROSS THE ROOM.* "Now let's try it out. Matt, come on up."

Matt held out the dryer and aimed the air at the ceiling. Then he propped the ball on top of the air. You know what? The ball floated. It just hung there in space, like magic.

Mr. Del Duca explained that the air moved symmetrically around the ball.

"Symmetrically?" asked Lindsey Boren, her pencil hovering over her notebook, quivering with her eagerness to write down the definition of a word she didn't know. Lindsey keeps a whole list of impressive words in the back of her notebook.

"Something is symmetrical if it's the same on both sides," explained Mr. Del Duca. "So the air held the ball in place the way airflow around an airplane keeps it steady."

Wow. That was even cooler than magic.

Another time we mixed glue, liquid starch, water, and borax—a type of detergent. It made silly putty. Who knew! We stretched it into different shapes, and I made myself a fake mustache that I wore the rest of the day. It was awesome!

We did an experiment every Friday using all kinds of ordinary stuff—eggs, vegetable oil, food coloring, a rolling pin. By the middle of October, we'd done four experiments.

The day my story begins, we were doing our fifth science experiment. As we walked into the classroom that morning, Super Matt jabbed me with his elbow.

"Check it out." Matt pointed to the table behind the teacher's desk where Mr. D had spread out the stuff for the experiment: paper cups (three rows of them), zip-lock baggies, a roll of paper towels. Under the table lay a thick stack of newspapers. We were going to do something cool for sure.

As soon as we finished morning attendance and math, Mr. D was ready to start science. He stood up front grinning and rocking on his heels the way he does when he thinks he has a spectacular idea. "Okay, team. Today"—Mr. D beat a drum roll in the air—"you're going to make Bubble Blasts!"

I flung my arms up. "I'm a Buzzy Blast. BAM! BOOM! POP!"

Mr. Del Duca rolled his eyes. "Cool it, Buzzy. Save your enthusiasm for the experiment. Okay, you'll be mixing chemicals, so you need safety goggles." He got the box of goggles off the shelf. "Lindsey, Amaya, you two can pass them out."

Lindsey came down the aisle, flipping out goggles. She dropped a pair on Cari's desk and a pair on mine.

"Thanks," said Cari.

"*De nada*," Lindsey replied.

"*De nada*" means "you're welcome" in

Spanish, and Lindsey loves to show off the fifteen words of Spanish she knows, even though Cari speaks English as well as anyone.

Caridad Perez moved here the second week of school because her mom got a job as a reporter on WKXR, the local TV station. Her mom's job must have rubbed off on Cari. She acts like she's a reporter, too.

I put my goggles on and waggled my fingers at Lindsey. "I'm Frog Man. Got any flies I can munch?" Lindsey made a face and kept going. That girl has no sense of humor.

"Today, you'll be working in teams," Mr. D said.

Frog poop! Since kindergarten, me and Jeff had been partners for everything. But this year, I'm in Mr. Del Duca's class, and Jeff is across the hall with Mrs. Ruiz. My mom said we goofed off too much in third grade. That's why we were split up.

"Pair up with the person who sits beside you. Row one with row two, three with four, and five with six."

Wait a minute. Cari Perez was sitting across from me. A girl! I was going to be stuck working with a girl. *Double frog poop!*

CHAPTER 2

MIXING UP THE CHEMICALS

I watched the other kids pair up. Super Matt and Dejon were a team. Lucky them.

"Don't make me work with a girl," I groaned. "Anything but that. I'll even work with Nibbles!"

"Put a lid on it, Buzzy," said Mr. D. So I was stuck with Cari, who thinks she's a TV news reporter.

Cari scooted her chair closer to my desk with the toe of her chunky black boot. She flipped back her dark hair and held her fist to her mouth, as if she was holding an imaginary microphone. "Speaking to you live from Mr. Del Duca's fourth grade class where Caridad Perez and Buzzy Baxter are about to make a Bubble Blast."

I rolled my eyes and looked back towards Mr. D.

"Today, my young science wizards," he said, "you'll see how different chemicals react when combined. On this table, I have paper cups filled with mysterious substances. Lindsey and Amaya, come up here and look in this cup. What do you think this powdery substance is?"

"Baby powder?" guessed Amaya.

"Flour?" guessed Lindsey.

"Good guesses, but no—it's actually baking soda. Okay, Lindsey," he continued, "smell the liquid in this cup. What do you think it is?"

"I know," said Lindsey smugly. "Vinegar. We use it to dye Easter eggs."

"Good." Mr. D smiled. "You're going to combine the two and see what happens. Each team, come get a baggie, a paper towel, and one paper cup each of vinegar, water, and baking soda." He spread a thick layer of newspapers on the floor as he talked.

"Yuck! The vinegar smells bad," said Super Matt.

"Stinky Slurpees!" I whispered loudly and made a gagging motion.

The boys snickered, the girls groaned. Mr. D shot me a stern look.

"We'll do the first Bubble Blast together. Lindsey and Amaya, you can do the demo for us."

Lindsey smiled.

"Lindsey, mix the vinegar and water in one cup. Now, Amaya," continued Mr. D, "pour the baking soda onto the paper towel. Fold the towel over and that's your time-release packet. In a minute we're going to pour the liquid into the plastic bag and drop in the packet. Dejon, what do you think will happen when the time release packet containing the baking soda is added to the vinegar and water?"

"These are Bubble Blasts. It'll blow up the school!" I burst out.

"Is your name Dejon?" Mr. Del Duca demanded.

"No," I mumbled.

"Dejon?"

"I think it will fizz a lot," Dejon said.

Mr. D wrote *MIXTURE WILL FIZZ* on the board. "Okay, let's find out," he continued. "Go ahead, girls."

Amaya dropped the packet into the plastic baggie. Lindsey zipped the bag and tossed it onto the newspapers. The bag began to fizz and puff up like a balloon filling with air. Bigger, bigger, POP! The bag burst, and liquid spilled over the newspapers.

"Wow!" said Lindsey.

"Cool!" exclaimed Amaya.

"Kablewy!" I yelled.

Mr. D grinned. "Pretty impressive, huh? Dejon's prediction was close. It fizzed as it puffed up and popped."

"Hey," I said, "Wouldn't it be cool to fill a giant trash bag! What a fizz-fest *that* would be!"

"Settle down, Buzzy." Mr. D turned back to the class. "Now, you're going to start your Bubble Blasts at your desks. Mix the vinegar and water in one cup and make your time-release packet. Then STOP until I call on you. One team at a time will come up to explode the Bubble Blasts. Okay, get to work."

"Mwahahaha!" I rubbed my hands together like a mad scientist. "Time for zee experiment."

As I mixed the water and vinegar, Cari spoke into her imaginary microphone. "We're at the laboratory of renowned scientist Buzzy Baxter. Tell me, Buzzy"—she stuck her imaginary microphone in my face—"what made you want to take up science?"

Maybe if I answered a few of her questions, she'd stop asking them. "Since I was a little kid, it's all I've dreamed about."

"How do you feel as you prepare to burst a Bubble Blast?"

"Like caterpillars are crawling around in my stomach." Actually my stomach was growling. I always get hungry around ten o'clock.

Cari put the baking soda on the paper towel and folded it up.

I was starving. Maybe I could sneak something out of my lunch.

"Dejon, Matt," Mr. D said. "You guys are up next."

Mr. D was going around the room in order. He wouldn't get to me and Cari for a while. I fished my lunch pack out of my desk and unzipped it on my lap. Peanut butter and jelly sandwich, vanilla pudding, a package of wheat crackers, a thermos of Grams' health juice.

Because my mom has to take it easy or the baby might come early, Grams has been packing my lunch. Grams is a health-nut. She even invented her own recipe for an energy drink she whips up in the blender. It's mostly vegetables and a packet of secret herbs she ordered online. Grams says that health juice gives her get-up-and-go. And I'll tell you this: my grandma definitely has get-up-and-go.

That got me wondering. If Grams' health juice and the Bubble Blast both produce energy, what would happen if I mixed them together? The paper cup that had held the baking soda had a thin layer caked in the bottom. I picked up the cup of vinegar and water and poured a few drops. The mixture began to fizz.

"What are you doing?" Cari demanded. "We need that liquid for our experiment."

"I only used a tiny bit. I want to see what happens if I add some of Grams' health juice."

I unscrewed the thermos and poured a dribble of Grams' juice into the paper cup.

Whoa! The mixture began to hiss and bubble. It swelled up inside the cup like it was about to overflow.

"Look out!" burst out Cari.

THE BUBBLE BLAST

"**A** volcano is erupting!" I exclaimed, watching the liquid almost spill over the cup.

Mr. Del Duca looked up from where Mei-Lin and Shawnda were exploding their bag. "Do you guys have a problem?"

I froze, waiting for Cari to rat on me.

"Uh," she said. "No. We're good."

"Well, quiet down until it's your turn." Mr. D turned back to Mei-Lin and Shawnda.

The fizzing had stopped. I scooped up a bit of the mixture on my pudding spoon and held it to my nose to take a sniff.

"Don't eat that, Buzzy!" Cari grabbed my arm.

"I'm not!" I yanked my hand away. The spoon flew from my fingers, flipping—like slow-motion—onto Nibbles' cage. Startled, he sat up as a few drops dripped through the bars and landed onto his paws.

With lightning speed, Nibbles licked up the liquid. My jaw dropped.

"Oh no!" Cari's eyes were round with horror. "Nibbles swallowed some of that . . . that . . . *stuff.*"

I stared at the hamster nervously. His bright eyes peered back at me. "He looks okay. I think he liked it. Vinegar and baking soda wouldn't hurt him, and my grandma's juice is made from fresh veggies. Mostly."

Plus that packet of secret herbs, I thought. Hopefully nothing that would hurt a hamster.

"Earth to Buzzy and Cari," called Mr. Del Duca. "Let's go."

Cari threw a nervous glance at Nibbles as we picked up our supplies and headed up front.

"Buzzy, pour in the vinegar mixture. Add the packet, Cari, and zip the bag shut."

Cari gave the bag a hard shake and tossed it onto the soggy newspapers.

"Ready for blast-off!" I shouted. "Four . . . three . . . two . . ."

BANG! The bag popped and water and vinegar gushed out.

I did a little victory dance. "That is so-o c-o-o-o-ol!"

"I thought you guys would enjoy this

experiment." Mr. D rubbed his hands.

Cari and I walked back to our seats, both glancing at Nibbles. He still seemed okay. Thank goodness.

Up front, Mr. D announced, "Time to clean up, everyone. After that, those of you who haven't presented your Me Museums yet can work on the autobiography part of the project. If you're done your autobiography, you can read a free-choice book. Either way, you're working quietly."

I slumped down in my seat. The dreaded Me Museum again. *Rat tails!* That project counted as a huge Language Arts grade. Huge! We had to put together a display of stuff related to our lives and write our autobiography to go with it. The display could include sports trophies, vacation souvenirs, family photos. Anything to show how interesting your life was.

Every Wednesday someone was scheduled to present their Me Museum. It was a big deal. Our whole family was invited to come and watch.

All I had so far was a stupid lock of my baby hair, a robin's egg I found in our yard, rocks and shells I had collected from different places, and a picture of me at the zoo in first grade. Big whoop!

My display was a bust. My autobiography? Even worse. I do *not* like to write. I have trouble coming up with one paragraph a week for my Language Arts journal. How was I supposed to write my whole life story? Especially when my life is pretty boring.

Most kids were already reading or scribbling away. Reluctantly, I got out my pencil and notebook. Maybe food would crank me up. I fished some wheat crackers out of my lunch, then glanced over at Nibbles, still a little worried. I sneaked a cracker into his cage and stuffed the others into my mouth.

Mr. Del Duca was walking around the room to check on kids. He stopped when he came to my desk. "How's that autobiography coming, Buzzy?"

"It's coming." Actually, I hadn't written one word since the last time he asked.

"When is it Buzzy's turn to present?" called Dejon from three rows up.

Mr. Del Duca consulted his chart. "Buzzy's scheduled for next Wednesday."

"It'll be hilarious," said Gunner. "Buzzy always rocks."

I knew they expected something special from me. For my space project last year, I wore an old Buzz Lightyear costume and a bike helmet wrapped in aluminum foil to look like a space helmet. I pretended I was floating in space, waving my arms and spinning around. I accidentally knocked the globe off Mrs. Shultz's desk. "Asteroid collision!" I yelled. Mrs. Shultz didn't think that was funny, but the kids did. They liked my social studies project too. I made up a song about the Wright brothers and folded a hundred airplanes. I brought the airplanes to school in a garbage bag. Then, during my presentation, I sang my song.

> *Oh, those good old Wright brothers,*
> *They went to Kitty Hawk*
> *They built themselves an airplane,*
> *To fly instead of walk.*
> *They built themselves an airplane,*
> *To zoom around the sky.*
> *Oh, those good old Wright brothers,*
> *they learned how to fly.*

The whole time I kept tossing out paper airplanes. They landed all over the classroom, and it took forever to pick them up. The kids loved it. But not Mrs. Shultz. She gave me a C on both projects.

This time, though, they were going to be disappointed. I had nothing funny or interesting to share. Nothing. Super Matt told about a time his family went camping and a bear ate their food. Dejon described bungee jumping with his uncle at Adventure Park. Amaya didn't have any great stories, but at least she has sisters that are triplets. What did I have? Diddly-squat.

My life was boring, boring, boring.

My mom had suggested I write about the new baby that was coming.

"What's exciting about that? People have babies all the time. Now if you and Dad had to rush to the hospital in the middle of the night, and a storm had washed out the bridge, and Dad had to take a detour, and the baby was born on the way, *that* would be exciting."

Mom rubbed her round stomach. "I am not having this baby in the car so that you can get a better grade, Buzzy."

So I was stuck with an autobiography that amounted to one-half page. Like I said, nothing exciting had ever happened to me.

Not yet.

CHAPTER 4

NIBBLES

The sound of scratching pencils came from around the room. The lucky kids who had already finished their autobiographies relaxed with their books at their desks or on our planet rug.

Mr. D was talking to Mei-Lin about her Me Museum. I chewed my pencil, trying desperately to think of something exciting to add.

"Disgusting."

"Huh?" I looked across the aisle at Cari. She was bent over her paper, concentrating.

"Absolutely disgusting."

That wasn't Cari's voice.

I turned the other way, toward the science table.

Inside the cage, Nibbles nudged with his nose the wheat cracker I'd given him. "This is the sorriest grub I ever ate."

The voice was coming from Nibbles!

"OHMIGOSH!" I yelled. People turned to look at me, laughing.

"Buzzy, do you have a problem?" asked Mr. Del Duca.

"No!" I blurted. "Not me. No problem."

"Then work. On. Your. Me Museum!" Mr. D chopped the sentence into little bits like he wanted to be sure I heard every word.

"Yes, Mr. Del Duca." I ducked my head and sneaked a sideways glance at Nibbles. Was I crazy? Nibbles pushed the cracker with his nose again. Then, without another word, he burrowed into the shavings.

Had I really heard the hamster talk?

I had. I knew I had.

My heart was jumping like a bouncy ball. I needed to tell someone or I'd go crazy. Jeff would believe me! I waved my hand at Mr. D and jerked my head toward the door.

When he nodded, I grabbed the bathroom pass and ran out.

Jeff's class was right across the hall. I walked past the open door. Mrs. Ruiz was writing on the board. I walked back, staring at Jeff. Come on, Jeff . . . look up! Finally, Jeff glanced my way. I waved for him to come

out to the hall. A minute later Jeff strolled out the door, carrying a bathroom pass.

I grabbed his arm and pulled him down the hall so no one in his class could hear us. "Jeff, you are *not* going to believe this," I whispered hoarsely. "Not in a million, trillion years."

Jeff's eyebrows popped up. "Mr. D said you're so smart, you never have to go to school again?" he teased.

"No."

"You won unlimited candy for the rest of your life?"

"No. Stop guessing." I put my hands on his shoulders and took a deep breath. "Nibbles can talk."

"What?"

"Nibbles. You know—our class hamster."

"That part I got. What did you say he could do?"

"He can *talk*."

Jeff stared at me like I had two noses. Then he burst out laughing. "You crack me up, Buzzy. How do you come up with these things? You've got the wildest imagination."

"I'm not kidding," I rushed on. "See, we were doing a science experiment. We had to mix up this concoction, and I added some of my grandma's health juice. I accidentally spilled some on Nibbles. He licked it off his fur, and a few minutes later, he talked."

"You're crazy, Buzzy." Jeff tilted his head, considering. "Okay, what did the talking hamster say?"

"He said, 'Disgusting!'"

"What?"

"He was talking about a cracker I slipped into his cage. Nibbles didn't like it. He said it was the sorriest grub he ever ate."

"Yeah, sure," said Jeff sarcastically. "That hamster's rehearsing for a show on the Food Channel. 'Rodents Rate Snacks,' maybe."

"I'll prove it to you. During lunch, we'll

sneak up to my classroom. You can hear Nibbles talk with your own ears."

"This better not be one of your jokes," Jeff warned. "Like the time when you told Lindsey Boren I thought she was cute, and she followed me around for days. If I walk into that classroom and find Lindsey waiting with puckered lips, you're *toast*."

"That was back in second grade." I backed towards my classroom door. "I'm telling the truth, Jeff. You'll see."

THE HAMSTER CAN TALK

When I got back into my classroom, Nibbles was still burrowed under the shavings. Sleeping, I guess. Had he really spoken? Or was I imagining it all?

Maybe I was hearing things. I snapped my fingers as loud as I could to make sure my ears were working.

"Buzzy." Mr. D gave me a frown and a headshake. My ears were working fine. Apparently his ears were, too.

The rest of the morning I kept an eye on Nibbles, hoping he'd say something else. But Nibbles stayed burrowed out of sight. Had he really talked? Maybe I'd heard another kid talking quietly and somehow thought it was Nibbles.

At lunchtime, I found Jeff at our usual table. He was stuffing a sandwich into his mouth with one hand, holding a carton of chocolate milk in the other hand. "Let me finish lunch, and then we can go visit your chatty hamster." He smirked at me.

Clearly he thought I was pulling something.

"Take your time," I told him. I was no longer in a rush to get up to the classroom.

"Don't worry, I'll be done in a second. I can't wait to hear Nibbles, the talking hamster."

It's hard to laugh while you're stuffing your face with a ham and cheese sandwich, but Jeff managed.

I barely ate half of my sandwich. I sniffed Grams' health juice but didn't drink any. As soon as Jeff finished, we went up to Mrs. Burman, the cafeteria monitor, and asked to go to the boys' room.

"Goodness, you boys must have inhaled your lunch," said Mrs. Burman. "Go ahead."

We sprinted around the corner and up the stairs to 4-D. I pushed open the door— and froze.

Cari was sitting beside the science table. She had pulled her chair over and was looking through a magnifying glass while she munched something from a plastic container.

"What are you doing here?" I demanded. "You're supposed to be in the cafeteria!"

"I told Mrs. Burman I was going to the bathroom and then I came up here. I wanted to make sure Nibbles was okay after he licked up that stuff you spilled in his cage." Cari adjusted the hamster's water bottle a tiny bit.

"You'll get in trouble," I told her.

"How?" Her shoulders lifted in a shrug. "No one will notice that I'm gone."

"What about the lunch buddy Mr. Del Duca assigned you?"

"Shawnda Jackson? After the first week, she asked if I'd mind if she ate with her regular friends. Anyway, what are *you* doing here? You're not allowed upstairs either."

Me and Jeff looked at each other. "We came to check on Nibbles, too."

"OK, people, I love the attention. But as you can see, I'm fine."

Our heads snapped toward the hamster cage. Nibbles crawled out of the shavings. He yawned and stretched his tiny paws.

"Whoa! That was incredible, Buzzy," Jeff said slowly. "How did you do it? Did you put a voice recorder under the cage?" He lifted the corner of the cage so he could peer under it.

"Stop!" Nibbles yelled. "You're tipping me over!"

Jeff's jaw dropped. Cari's eyes got as big as tennis balls.

"Am I dreaming?" whispered Jeff as he set the cage down. "Or is that hamster really talking?"

"If it's a dream, I'm having it too," Cari said.

I punched Jeff's arm. "I *told* you Nibbles could talk." I could hardly believe it myself—but at least now I knew I wasn't crazy.

Nibbles stood on his hind legs, his front paws together. He stared at us with his shiny brown eyes.

"Why, so I can," said Nibbles. "Talk, I mean." He looked surprised too. "I wonder if I can sing as well." He gave a little cough and put his paw to his chest.

> *O-oh say can you see by the dawn's early light,*
> *What so proudly we hailed at the twilight's last gleaming.*

His voice was a little thin, but he really belted out the notes.

"This is *weird*," Jeff breathed. "A hamster that can sing ' The Star-Spangled Banner.'"

"What's so weird about that?" Nibbles asked. "I hear it every morning during announcements. And quit calling me 'the hamster.' I have a name."

"It's either a miracle or a scientific break-through!" said Jeff. "You made him talk."

"*You* made him talk?" said Cari, staring at me.

"Not me. Our science experiment," I said. "The Bubble Blast. He started talking after he licked that stuff off his fur."

"Whoa . . ." Cari tapped her nails on the table top, thinking. "Baking soda and vinegar? Nothing odd there. It must have been your grandma's health juice that did the trick. Remember how it made the experiment fizz up even more? That health juice must be powerful stuff."

Nibbles was burrowing under the wood shavings again, his furry bottom disappearing fast.

"Don't go, Nibbles," I said hastily, trying to think of a topic he'd want to talk about. "Uh, so you're not wild about wheat crackers. What do you like to eat?"

Nibbles' nose poked up from the shavings, his eyes bright. "I'm glad you asked. The Goldfish crackers you give me are yummy. But the seed mix I get every day—that's boring. I miss the treats Cowboy Bob fed us at Pet Corral."

"Pet Corral?" I said. "The pet store downtown?"

"You betcha! That's where I was born, pardners." Nibbles' brown eyes glistened. "Cowboy Bob ran the place. He fed us good grub and played great country music all day long. I had ten brothers and sisters, but they all got sold before me." Nibbles sighed longingly.

"Unbelievable," said Jeff. "The world's only talking hamster. Right here at Filbert Elementary School."

"I told you," I reminded him.

"I thought you made it up. Or flipped your lid."

"Can you picture everyone's faces when they find out Nibbles can talk?"

Jeff shook his head. "They'll be in total shock."

"Wait a minute," said Cari. "Maybe we shouldn't tell anyone."

"Are you crazy? Why not?" I demanded.

"Think about it." Cari scrunched her nose. "We tell the class. Kids rush home and tell their parents. Someone right away calls WKXR News. They send over a camera crew and a reporter. This is the kind of story my mom covers."

"So? What's wrong with being on television?" *We'll be famous,* I thought. *Sweet.*

Cari shook her head slowly. "Once people find out Nibbles can talk, they'll want to do experiments on him."

"What people?" said Jeff. "Mr. Del Duca?"

Cari shook her head. "Scientists. People from the government. Did you ever watch E.T.? Remember when the scientists invaded the boy's home and hooked E.T. up to all those tubes?"

I imagined Nibbles strapped to a laboratory table, a leather cuff around each paw, a bright light shining into his face. "My little sister Max freaked out at that part," I said.

"After the experiments are over," Cari continued, "someone will want to exhibit him in a museum or send him around in a traveling circus."

I pictured Nibbles shut up inside a glass case or trapped behind bars while people gawked at him. Not a happy picture.

Maybe Cari was right.

"Listen up, guys." Nibbles put his paws together. "All that conversation about food has made me hungry."

"Give him something to eat from your lunch, Buzzy," said Jeff.

"That's what started this whole thing, pea brain. My lunch."

"Not your grandma's health juice. Give him part of your sandwich."

I fished out the remains of my PB&J sandwich. Nibbles sniffed the squashed piece I broke off for him. Then he took a bite. "Not bad. Anything else?"

"I have some chicken and rice left." Cari opened the plastic container and poked a small piece of chicken stuck with a few grains of rice into Nibbles' cage. Nibbles took a cautious taste then gobbled up the whole thing.

"Yummy-yum-yum!" His tongue flicked a dab from his mouth. "Got any more?"

"You should be eating vegetables and seeds," I told him. "That's what the hamster handbook said."

"Ptooey!" Nibbles spat out the word. "That book is crazy as popcorn on a hot skillet. Would you want to live on a diet of vegetables and seeds?"

"No doughnuts?" said Jeff. "No pizza? Never? Painful."

"Well, an occasional treat's okay," I agreed. "But only once in a while."

"A treat," interrupted Nibbles. "That's what I need. Something sweet."

"There's nothing else in my lunch, but I know just the thing." I hustled up to Mr. Del Duca's desk, where he kept a jar full of different kinds of snacks. The Awesome Treat Jar, he calls it. Whenever someone did something outstanding, Mr. D would say, "Good job! Help yourself to something from the Awesome Treat Jar."

A hamster who talked deserved an Awesome Treat. I fished around in the jar, wondering whether Nibbles would rather have fruit chews or a mini granola bar.

"Mr. Baxter! What do you think you're doing?"

Mr. Del Duca stood in the doorway, frowning. *Hoppin' hamsters!* I was up to my elbow in the treat jar.

"I was, uh . . . getting an Awesome Treat for . . . um . . . um . . ."

"For Cari," said Jeff loudly.

"Yes, for Cari. Because . . . because . . ." I pulled out a pack of fruit chews.

"Because she gave up her lunch period to keep an eye on Nibbles," Jeff put in. "Don't you think she deserves an Awesome Treat?"

"What's wrong with Nibbles?" Mr. D crossed to the back of the room and peered into the hamster cage. "He looks fine."

I returned to the science table, holding the fruit chews.

"Nibbles was trembling during the science experiment," Cari said. "I think the noise scared him. So I came up early to make sure he was okay."

"That was nice of you, Cari," said Mr. D. "Give her the fruit chews, Buzzy, but from now on, remember: I'm in charge of dispensing treats."

As I handed Cari the fruit chews, Jeff, Cari, and I stared at each other, scared that Nibbles might suddenly burst out with a protest.

THE GIGANTIC SOCKS

As we stood there, staring nervously at Nibbles, the bell rang. One o'clock, the end of lunch. Footsteps thumped on the stairs, and kids started coming into the classroom. Cari and Jeff still stood there, eyes glued on Nibbles.

Mr. D scooped up a piece of scrap paper from the floor. He fired the crumpled paper at the trash can. *Swish.* "Buzzy, Cari, take your seats. Jeff, were you thinking of joining our class?"

Jeff jerked his head around. "Can I?" he asked hopefully.

"Nope. It would break Mrs. Ruiz's heart if you left her class."

"Okay, I'm outta here," Jeff said. He backed toward the door, never taking his eyes off the hamster cage.

Up front, Mr. Del Duca rapped on his desk to get our attention. "Eyes up front, everybody. Buzzy, that includes you."

I reluctantly pulled my attention from Nibbles and tried to focus on Mr. D.

"All right, team. First item on the afternoon agenda is Lindsey's Me Museum. Dejon and Matt, please set up chairs for Lindsey's mom and dad. Lindsey, will your Aunt Ellen be joining us?" Mr. Del Duca looked at Lindsey, who was arranging her Me Museum stuff on a table up front.

"No, she has a deadline to meet. She writes for *Sports for Kids*, and she's working on a story on some basketball player. Lawrence Clayburn. I think that's his name."

Lawrence Clayburn! That pried my attention away from Nibbles. Lawrence Clayburn was my favorite athlete in the entire world. Lindsey hardly knew his name, and her aunt got to interview him!

Other kids recognized him too. I heard whispers: "Lawrence Clayburn? Wow! He's the greatest."

Lindsey rummaged in her pink cloth bag and brought out a rolled-up white lump. "My aunt told Mr. Clayburn that her niece—me—

loves basketball and asked if she could have a souvenir for me. He gave her these socks."

Lindsey shook out a pair of ribbed athletic socks. The biggest socks I had ever seen in my life. As long as my arm. Longer.

I thought I'd have a heart attack. Lindsey wasn't a basketball fan. She barely knew what a basketball was! But the kids were eating it up. "Cool!" "Sweet!" "Awesome!"

"Oh, man," exclaimed Super Matt. "How would you like to hang that sock over your fireplace on Christmas Eve?"

Lindsey hadn't even begun her presentation, and already everyone was crazy about it. I couldn't match her Me Museum unless I came in riding on a kangaroo with a crown of Fourth of July sparklers blazing on my head.

Even Mr. D was practically drooling. "That's one famous pair of socks you have there, Lindsey. Okay," he looked around the room, "who's the announcer for today? Caridad, right?"

Cari didn't answer.

I glanced over and saw Cari staring toward Nibbles in a daze. Her unopened pack of fruit chews lay on her desk.

"Cari!" I hissed and poked her shoulder.

"So, Cari, you're the announcer," Mr. D repeated.

"Oh, uh, yeah."

"We'll start as soon as Lindsey's parents arrive, so be prepared. While we wait, somebody tell me again—what's the difference between a biography and an autobiography?"

Amaya raised her hand. "An autobiography is when you write a story about your own life. A biography is when you write the story of somebody else's life."

"Excellent, Amaya."

At 1:15 on the dot, Lindsey's parents knocked on the door. Dejon, who was the greeter this time, let them in. "Welcome to 4-D," he said and gave a bow.

Mrs. Boren looked the way I could picture Lindsey as a grownup: brown hair, glasses, and prissed up mouth. Lindsey's dad kept tugging at his tie to loosen it, and he spilled over the sides of the little chair when he sat down.

Cari marched up front. She shook her head, her black hair flying, like she was trying to clear her head.

"*Hola*. Good afternoon. I'm Caridad Perez, here in Mr. Del Duca's fourth grade classroom at Filbert Elementary School. As we bring you live coverage of Lindsey Boren's Me Museum, I'd like to welcome our guests, Mr. and Mrs. Boren. Lindsey, the stage is yours."

"Great job, Cari," said Mr. D. "Lindsey worked hard preparing her Me Museum. I know you'll be good listeners."

He looked right at me when he said that part. I shot a sideways glance at Nibbles. The hamster was sitting on his haunches, front paws together, his brown eyes watching Lindsey. I hoped *he* would be a good listener.

Lindsey opened a folder that had gold stars stuck to the cover and began, "My name is Lindsey Charlotte Boren. I was born on November eighteenth. My mother says I was a very pretty baby."

"She was. She had beautiful curls," called out Lindsey's mom. "She was such a sweet baby, too," Mrs. Boren went on. "Never fussed."

Never fussed, I thought. *Lindsey must have been saving it up, 'cause she sure does complain a lot now.*

"This was my first baby dress"—Lindsey held up a dress with ruffles on the skirt and pink butterflies on the top—"and my first pair of shoes." Lindsey waved the little pair of baby shoes.

It was hard to imagine that Lindsey's big feet ever fit inside those little tiny shoes.

The girls all went "Awwww" while a couple of boys rolled their eyes. I wanted to puke.

But then a loud snicker came from my corner of the room.

Mr. D gave me a stern glance. The hair on my neck prickled. *Creepin' caterpillars!* That wasn't me snickering at Lindsey's baby shoes.

It was Nibbles.

I shot the hamster a warning look, but he ignored me. He was busy watching Lindsey.

Please, Nibbles, keep quiet, I thought.

Instead, Nibbles began to sing, his squeaky voice just loud enough to be heard across the room. "*Ohhhhhhh, my sweet Prairie Rose, with your tiny toes . . .*"

Lindsey glared at me over her baby shoes and so did her parents and Mr. D. "Buzzy," he hissed. "What did I tell you about being a good listener? Pipe down."

I started coughing, to cover up. It was pointless. I was famous for making smart-aleck comments. Who would believe it was the hamster singing and not me?

Lindsey then picked up a book. "*Good-night Moon* was my first book. My parents read to me every night and played classical music while I napped. Maybe that's why I started talking when I was only ten months old."

"And never stopped," muttered the same voice. That wisecracking hamster couldn't keep his comments to himself!

Most of the boys were busting up.

Mr. D had had it. "All right, Buzzy. Up here by my desk!" he snapped.

As I stood up, Nibbles vanished under a pile of wood shavings. Too bad I couldn't do the same.

I carried my chair up to Mr. D's desk and sat down. "It wasn't me," I whispered feebly. "Honest."

"Save it," he said, his eyes shooting sparks at me. "I'm sorry, Lindsey. You can go on now."

I almost wished Nibbles would stand up and holler, *"Hey. It was me. Back here, guys,"* but nothing stirred in the pile of shavings.

After Lindsey finished and everyone got to hold the famous socks, her parents left—but not before her mom shot me a poisonous look. Mr. D told the class to open their Social Studies books and start reading chapter eight. Then he turned to me. "You. Out in the hall."

I felt like limp spaghetti. It is *very* scary to have Mr. Del Duca mad at you.

Out in the hall, Mr. D cornered me behind the open door. "What's up with you, Buzzy?" he said in a loud whisper. "Lindsey worked hard on her Me Museum, and you did your best to spoil it. Is that how you want people to act when you do your presentation?"

"No. It's not how I want people to act." *Or hamsters*, I thought, looking down at my sneakers.

"You have a good sense of humor, Mr. Baxter. But there's a time and a place for funny comments. You need to learn when to keep your mouth shut. Now, how do you think you should handle this situation?"

How should I handle it? I should tie a little gag on that hamster! But I knew that wasn't the answer Mr. D wanted to hear. "I should apologize," I mumbled.

"Right. Now you're using good sense."

The thought of apologizing to Lindsey was torture. "Can I write her a note instead?" I asked in a small voice.

"I think writing an apology note would be a good idea," he agreed. "It'll give you a chance to choose the right words."

Everyone looked up as we came back inside, expecting to see my head chopped off or something. I took a piece of paper from my desk and wrote,

Dear Lindsey,

I'm sorry for the wizecracks made during your Me Museum. You worked hard to get ready. Nothing should have interrupted your presentation.

From Buzzy

I stared at the note, frustrated. *Oh, man,* I thought. It was bad enough apologizing when I did something wrong. Now I had to apologize for something done by a hamster!

Lindsey sniffed when she read my note. "You're the worst speller in the world, Buzzy. Wisecracks should be spelled with an 's'. You probably can't even spell your own name."

I went back to my desk and slumped in my seat. Done in by a talking hamster. Speaking of the hamster, I glanced over at him. I'd been so busy dealing with the Lindsey problem, I forgot how excited I was that he could talk!

Right before three o'clock, Mr. D wadded up a piece of paper and waved it in the air. "Okay, team, if I miss this shot, you can skip your Social Studies homework tonight." He turned and fired the paper ball at the trash can. *Swish.*

"You never miss," grumbled Dejon.

"Good thing!" Mr. D grinned. "Because homework is important. Pack up, bell's about to ring."

When it did ring, kids streamed out of the room—except me and Cari. I was trying to take as long as I could to pack up so Mr.

D would leave and I could talk to Nibbles. It looked like Cari was doing the same.

"Buzzy, Cari, school's over. Get moving," said Mr. D.

Rat droppings! He wasn't going to leave until we did. Reluctantly I zipped my backpack and gave one final glance at the hamster cage. Nibbles was buried under a pile of shavings. Resting up for his next performance, maybe?

I followed Cari out the door. Jeff was waiting in the hall.

"Wait till I tell you what Nibbles did," I groaned. I told him the whole story.

"That's hilarious," he kept saying. "But, wait a minute," he said when he finished laughing. "Did you say Lindsey had Lawrence Clayburn's socks?"

"Will you two stop talking about a stupid pair of socks," Cari interrupted. "We need to figure out what to do about Nibbles."

I took a deep breath. "I've been thinking. You might be right, Cari—about people wanting to experiment on Nibbles. Or put him in a circus."

"So we're going to keep it a secret?"

I nodded.

"What about our parents?" asked Jeff.

"We should make a pact that we won't tell them—or anyone," Cari insisted. She stuck out her hand. Jeff and me put ours on top.

"We swear not to tell that Nibbles can talk," Cari said solemnly.

"We swear not to tell that Nibbles can talk," me and Jeff repeated.

"Cross my heart, spit in my eye, break this oath, I hope to die."

We repeated it.

There was silence for a second. Then I said, "The one who should really be taking a vow of silence is Nibbles."

CHAPTER 7

SNEAKING INTO SCHOOL

The rest of the day, I felt ready to burst. I was carrying around this incredible news, and I couldn't tell anyone. Grams made spaghetti for dinner. Watching her stir the bubbling pot, I wondered whether she had any idea how powerful her health juice was.

At the dinner table, Dad asked, "Anything special happen at school today, Buzz?"

Yeah! Our class hamster sang "The Star-Spangled Banner" and insulted my classmate. The words almost jumped from my mouth. Instead I twisted worms of spaghetti around my fork and said, "Just the usual. Lunch was good. Peanut butter and jelly sandwich and Grams' yummy health juice."

I watched for Grams' reaction.

"Why, Buzzy, I'm glad you liked it."

48

Grams winked at me. "Full of vitamins to make you strong."

Did she know what power the drink had when it got mixed with a few other ingredients? I couldn't tell.

I was so nervous, I barely finished my spaghetti and couldn't concentrate on my homework. Questions bounced in my head. What if I got to school tomorrow and Nibbles had stopped talking? Worse, what if I walked in and found him chatting away to Mr. D? I could see Mr. D's jaw hanging down. I could see guys in white coats bursting into the classroom, hauling Nibbles away.

In the morning, I gobbled up my scrambled eggs and ran outside.

"Hey!" It was Jeff hurrying toward me waving waffles wrapped in a paper towel. "I couldn't wait," he said, "So I brought my breakfast to-go."

"I know!" I agreed. "I'm dying to see if Nibbles can still talk."

"Let's go," he said, shoving a hunk of waffle in his mouth.

We jogged all the way to school, but as early as we were, Cari beat us to it.

"Hi," she greeted us. "I can't wait to get

in to see Nibbles. What if we imagined the whole thing?"

"All three of us imagining the same thing? No chance," I said. But inside, my stomach butterflies were doing the dance of doubt.

Jeff didn't say anything. He was too busy stuffing the last bit of waffle into his mouth.

Cari spoke into her imaginary microphone, the words spilling out as fast as she could move her mouth. "This is Caridad Perez live on the scene at Filbert Elementary School, where we are ready to learn whether Nibbles, the talking hamster, can still talk."

"I can't stand the wait," I groaned. "Let's go in now."

"We're not allowed," Cari pointed out. "The playground aide won't let us in."

"Ouch! Oww! I just twisted my ankle. Hey, guys, help me get to the nurse." I winked.

"Ah, the old injured ankle trick," said Jeff. "Good thinking."

I flung an arm around each of them, and we hobbled over to the aide. "Buzzy hurt his ankle. Can we take him to the nurse?" Cari asked.

"Buzzy, are you okay? Sure, kids, go ahead."

We went in the front door. Inside, I could see Mrs. Jackson, the secretary, typing away at her computer. She looked up at us.

"Buzzy hurt his ankle," Cari explained. "We're taking him to the nurse."

"Okay, kids." She sipped from her coffee mug and waved us on.

As we reached the stairs, my ankle made an amazing recovery. We raced upstairs and skidded to a halt outside Mr. D's room. I peeked in. No sign of the big guy. He was probably in the teachers' room getting his coffee.

We hurried to the science table. Nibbles was asleep under the shavings. "Hey, Nibbles," I whispered.

"Wake up, little hamster." Jeff rattled the cage.

The mound of shavings quivered. Nibbles crawled out, small curls of wood stuck to his fur. "Doesn't anybody care that I'm trying to sleep?" he demanded indignantly.

Cari, Jeff, and I high-fived each other. "He can still talk!" I exclaimed.

"Of course I can talk," said Nibbles. "Quite well, too, if I do say so myself."

"Sorry we woke you," Cari apologized.

Nibbles twitched his nose. "Now that I'm up, did you bring me any treats? Something tasty from your lunch maybe?"

"We'll bring you treats later," Cari replied. "I promise."

I bent close to the cage. "Nibbles, we have something important to tell you. You can't let anyone know you can talk. Except us. You have to keep . . . very . . . quiet."

Nibbles rubbed his eyes. "You woke me up to tell me that?"

"Sorry. We—"

The sound of the bell drowned me out. When it stopped, I begged, "Just, please, be quiet."

Footsteps clattered in the hall, and kids came pushing into class. Mr. Del Duca came in carrying a tall mug of coffee. "Good morning, gang," he called, dropping a pile of papers on his desk.

Lindsey slid her backpack onto her chair and came to the science table. "How did you three get in here already?" she asked suspiciously.

"We're working on a special project," Cari told her.

"What special project?" asked Lindsey, clearly bothered by the thought of us doing extra work.

"Buzz and Cari, are you going to wear your backpacks all day or unpack them and join us?" Mr. D straightened his tie, the one with basketballs printed all over it.

"We're going to join you," said Cari. She thumped her backpack to the floor and took off her jacket.

I gave Nibbles an anxious look, hoping he had gotten the message.

"Jeff, we love having you on our team, but I don't think Mrs. Ruiz is ready to give you up just yet."

"Right." Jeff gave me a worried look and left the room.

Cari and I unpacked our backpacks and went to hang them up.

"I hope Nibbles got the message and keeps his mouth shut," I told her quietly.

When we were all at our desks, Mr. D said, "Okay, sports fans, let's get this day started."

As Mr. D took attendance and lunch count, Amaya watered the plants, and Dejon wrote today's date on the board.

"Everyone, put your math homework in the bin," Mr. D said.

Math homework. I'd forgotten all about homework last night. *Rat tails!* We got two points off for every missing assignment.

Apart from that, the morning started off okay. Nibbles slept straight through to Social Studies.

Then, the trouble started.

"We're going to continue our discussion of our town government this morning. First we'll review a bit. Who can tell me the name of the mayor?"

Amaya's hand shot up. "Judith Robinette."

"Right. And who works with the mayor to govern the town, Lindsey?"

"The board of commissioners. The board has six members, and they meet once a month."

"Excellent. You guys are cookin' today! Where do the commissioners meet?"

"The Coffee Café." I didn't mean to say that. It just popped out.

Mr. D gave me The Look. "Don't call out, Buzzy. Raise your hand. And the commissioners do not meet at the Coffee

Café. Why would you think that?"

"My dad says he sees them there so much, there must be café lattes in the town budget."

A few people laughed. Lindsey groaned and tapped her pencil on her desk.

"All right, Buzzy. That's enough."

I heard a sound to my side and looked over at Nibbles' cage. He was waking up, stretching his little paws. *Uh oh,* I thought.

CHAPTER 8

THE HAMSTER-NAPPING PLOT

First I heard humming. Then a familiar voice sang softly, *"Git along little doggies, git along."* I glanced over. Nibbles was lying on his back, paws pedaling the air.

I shot him a glare and wiggled my eyebrows.

"I'm exercising," he whispered loudly.

I shook my head at him. Nibbles got the message—but up front, Mr. D was frowning in my direction again. "Buzzy, did you have something else to say?"

I gave him my innocent look. "Who me? Not me. My lips are buttoned. Tight as a drum."

He held up his hand. "Keep it that way. Now, can someone please tell me where the commissioners meet?"

Lindsey raised her hand. "They meet at Borough Hall, Mr. Del Duca. That big brick building on Main Street."

"Burrow. Did someone say burrow? We hamsters love to burrow." *Uh-oh.*

Mr. Del Duca sent me a look that would punch holes in concrete. "Buzzy, what did I just tell you about not calling out!"

"It wasn't me," I stammered. I saw Cari lift her eyebrows to give me a warning. "I mean, uh, yes it was me. I had a question. And it just popped out before I remembered to raise my hand."

Mr. D tossed the chalk from one hand to the other. "And the question was?"

"I . . . um . . ." Think, think. Ask something. Anything. "Does the mayor live in Borough Hall?"

Kids burst out laughing, and I felt my face turn red.

Mr. D rubbed his forehead like he couldn't take much more of this. "All right, Buzzy, you know the answer is no. Now just stop calling out, okay?"

When Mr. D wasn't looking, I glanced at Nibbles. Did that hamster look sorry for the trouble he'd just caused? No, he did not. If it's possible for a hamster to shrug his shoulders, that's what Nibbles did. Then he drank from his water bottle, stepped onto his exercise wheel, and began to run.

Lunchtime followed social studies. Nibbles was napping by then. I grabbed my lunch bag and raced to the cafeteria. I sat waiting at our usual table while Jeff worked his way through the lunch line. He slid his tray, loaded with French toast and syrup, pudding, and canned fruit, onto the table.

"How'd it go with you-know-who?" he asked softly.

"Not too bad at first," I whispered. "Nibbles was asleep."

Jeff always ate his dessert first. Yummy-looking chocolate pudding with whipped cream on top. I unwrapped my PB&J on wheat bread.

"But then Nibbles woke up . . ."

Jeff shoveled pudding into his mouth, his eyes fixed on me.

". . . and the next thing I know, he's exercising and singing some country song. Then he started in with the comments! That little guy can't let two seconds go by without a smart-aleck comment. He's driving me crazy."

Jeff choked back a laugh and pointed his plastic spoon at me. "He sounds like you."

"*Hola!* Is anybody sitting here?"

We looked up. Cari stood by the table, holding her lunch pack.

"Yeah, my sweatshirt is." Jeff pointed to the sweatshirt he'd dropped on the chair.

"Is it okay if I move it? *Si?*" Without waiting for an answer, Cari put Jeff's sweatshirt on the next chair and sat down.

Jeff and I rolled our eyes at each other, and I shrugged. "Who cares? She already knows he can talk."

Cari unzipped her lunch pack.

"Listen," I began, "I thought of something important. We can't leave Nibbles in school over the weekend. What if Mr. Pete the custodian comes in to clean our classroom, and Nibbles starts making wisecracks?"

"You're right. That would be a catastrophe." Cari bit her lip.

"Nibbles can come home with me," Jeff offered.

"You have Patch," I said as I shoved the last bite of PB&J into my mouth.

"Dogs chase cats, not hamsters, and Patch is too lazy to chase anything." Jeff dipped some French toast in syrup and stuffed it into his mouth.

"My mom won't let me have any kind of pet," said Cari. "She says she doesn't have time to take care of an animal because she works such long hours."

"So then Nibbles should come home with me," I said. "I'll ask Mr. Del Duca if I can take him for the weekend."

"Sounds like a plan," said Jeff.

Cari held up her cup of fruit. "I'll take some of this to Nibbles. I promised him I'd bring him something to eat."

When the lunch bell rang, we hurried upstairs. Cari slid a few pieces of fruit into Nibbles' dish. "Yummy-yum-yum! Thanks," he whispered.

First thing after lunch, Mr. D had us do problems from our math books, while he went up and down the aisles giving individual help. When he reached my desk, he asked, "Any questions, Buzz?"

"Yeah. Can I take Nibbles home for the weekend?"

He tapped on my forehead. "Knock knock, anybody home? We're doing math, Buzzy. Remember math? Little numbers you multiply and divide? Anyway, Nibbles stays in school over weekends. I told you guys that back in September. Over longer holidays, like Thanksgiving and Christmas, someone will have to take him home."

I rolled my pencil in my hands and thought fast. "I'll bet Nibbles gets lonely here by himself all weekend long."

"Hamsters are solitary animals, Buzz. They enjoy time alone. Kind of like teachers." Mr. D laughed at his own joke. "I'm kidding. I love having you guys around."

Toad poop! Now what?

Cari shot me a quick look, her eyebrows flickering. I figured she'd overheard the conversation.

After math we watched the movie *Charlotte's Web* for Language Arts. Nibbles slept the whole time. I'd always wished the little hamster stayed awake more during the day. Now I was glad he spent so much time catching zzzz's. Saved me from worrying that he'd pop out more crazy comments.

Finally the three o'clock bell rang. In the hall, I grabbed my backpack and put on my sweatshirt. I watched for Jeff to leave Mrs. Ruiz's classroom. I grabbed his arm and pulled him close to the wall, away from the mob of kids flowing down the hall. "Mr. D said I can't take Nibbles home," I said.

"That stinks with a capital S," he replied. "Now what?"

"That leaves us no other choice," I said dramatically. "We've gotta kidnap the little guy!"

CHAPTER 9

THE HULK

Jeff snickered. "Kidnap? Don't you mean hamster-nap?"

"Whatever you call it, we've got to do it—smuggle Nibbles out of here."

Jeff wasn't so easily convinced. "Mr. D said you couldn't take the hamster home, so you want us to sneak in and snatch him? Do you want us to get a hundred days detention?"

"Can you say 'emergency'? If we leave Nibbles here, he's bound to say hello to Mr. Pete when he's scrubbing desks. Remember what Cari said. If people find out Nibbles can talk, he's going end up as a science experiment or in the circus."

Jeff nodded slowly. "You're right. Okay— one hamster-napping coming up."

"Mr. D always scrams outta here pretty

quick on Fridays. As soon as he leaves, we'll grab Nibbles."

We ducked into the boys' bathroom to kill time and spent a few minutes shooting wadded-up paper towels at the trash can. Finally, I eased the door open and peeked out. The hall was empty.

"Coast is clear. Let's move."

As we started up the hall, a voice from behind called softly, "Wait!" I spun around and saw Cari just leaving the girls' bathroom.

"You were spying," I accused.

Cari gave me the evil eye. "News flash. You forgot to tell me what's going on. I know you're up to something. You left without Nibbles, and you rushed out of the classroom like your pants were on fire."

To tell the truth, worrying over Nibbles, I had forgotten all about Cari. "We're hamster-napping Nibbles," I admitted. "Since Mr. D wouldn't let me take him home."

She thought for a minute, then said, "I can help."

I couldn't think of any way to get rid of Cari so I let her follow us back to Mr. Del Duca's room. Empty.

Nibbles was nibbling food from his hamster dish. He looked up and twitched his nose. "Seeds, seeds, and more seeds. Do you have any idea how bored I am with plain old seeds? I long for an apple, even a carrot to chew. But no-o-o-o-o," his voice rolled. "All I get are these dumb seeds."

"I'm taking you home for the weekend," I told him. "I'll find you something better to eat at my house."

"Mr. D said nix on that idea, pardner. I heard him."

"Right, that's why we're going to hamster-nap you."

"What?" cried Nibbles.

"How are we going to get the cage out?" Jeff asked suddenly. "We might run into someone in the halls."

Frog poop! I hadn't thought of that. I pictured us running into Mrs. Ruiz carrying our class hamster cage. How would we explain that one? "Maybe we could tie a rope around the cage and lower it out the window," I suggested.

"Forget that." Nibbles put his little paws over his eyes. "Heights scare me!"

"Besides, we don't have a rope," Jeff

pointed out.

"Mr. D's got a bunch of extra ties stashed in his desk. We could tie some of his ties together."

"Buzzy, that's a crazy idea. *Loco!* Kids on the playground would see the cage coming down," Cari objected.

"You guys so much as open that window," sniffed Nibbles, "and I'll scream bloody murder."

Cari snapped her fingers. "News flash—we don't need the cage. You can carry Nibbles in your pocket. Then we'll make him a home out of a box at your house."

"Great idea!" said Jeff. "If the cage is here and anyone hunts for the hamster, it'll look like Nibbles just escaped."

"Forget it," said Nibbles.

"Why?" Jeff asked.

"Would you want to crawl into Buzzy's pocket?"

"What's wrong with my pocket?" I demanded, insulted, looking down at the kangaroo pocket on the front of my sweatshirt.

Jeff smirked. "I guess Nibbles doesn't want to get squashed in with already-chewed gum and used tissues."

"I don't carry gross stuff around in my pockets. Look." I slid up the cage door so Nibbles could sniff his way out. I dug into my pocket and pulled out a plastic spider. "Nothing gross about that."

Nibbles nodded. "The spider's okay."

Next out, a few tissues.

"I told you he'd have tissues in there," Jeff hooted.

"They're clean." I waved them in Jeff's face. "My grandma makes me carry them in case I have a sneezing fit."

The next thing I dropped on the table caught Nibbles' attention. It was a half-eaten bag of Skittles, and a few spilled out of the bag.

"They look tasty." Nibbles licked one. "Mmm, yummy-yum-yum!"

"Hey, my Skittles! I was saving them for later. But they're all yours now that you've licked them."

I pulled out a marble. "Oh-h-h," cried Nibbles. "More candy."

"Hold it, hamster!" I shoved a hand in front of the greedy guy's mouth. "That's not candy—it's my lucky marble."

"I guess it can stay," Nibbles said. "Too bad it's not edible."

I fished out a small rock. "I found this in my yard. Cool, huh? Doesn't it look like a fossil?"

"It could crush my paws," said Nibbles.

"I'll hold it for you," Jeff offered. He dropped the rock into his pocket.

"Ready?" I picked Nibbles up. Gently, very gently, I slipped him into my sweatshirt pocket.

Cari spoke into her imaginary microphone. "Coming to you live from the scene of the hamster-napping, this is Cari Perez, here with Buzzy Baxter and Jeff Woodhouse. The boys are about to sneak Nibbles out of the school. Do you have something to say, Buzzy?"

"Let's scram," I said. "We're wasting time!"

We hurried along the hall and down the stairs. I kept a hand over my pocket so I wouldn't jiggle Nibbles too much. We were heading for the front door when a voice behind us called out, "Whoa!"

Our principal, Mr. Marcozi, stood there. I couldn't think of a worse person to run into.

"Hey, you three. Stop right there." Mr. Marcozi came toward us, straightening his tie. "What's the rule about running in the hall, Buzzy?"

"Run on the right?" I guessed hopefully. It was worth a try.

"No-o-o-o," said Mr. Marcozi, looking irritated.

I couldn't resist another attempt at humor. "Run in single file?"

I saw Mr. Marcozi's shoulders stiffen. He'd lost patience, the way Mr. Del Duca does when I keep goofing off.

"No, Mr. Baxter. The rule about running

is, *don't do it.* Not on the right. Not in single file. Not at all. No running."

When people call you "Mr. Baxter," you know you're in trouble.

"Sorry, Mr. Marcozi," Cari said sweetly. "We won't do it again."

"Thank you, Caridad." Mr. Marcozi nodded. "You three may go. But walk."

We walked down the hall so slowly it was painful and then stepped out the door into the fall sunshine. I was sweating inside my sweatshirt. Lots of kids were hanging around, playing. As we hustled past the playground, I peeked into my pocket. "Nibbles, you okay?"

"Buzz," Jeff warned. "Look out!"

Too late.

I had just crashed into a wall. Not an actual wall—Adrienne Archer, the biggest, meanest safety patroller in the fifth grade. Me and Jeff call her the Hulk. Not to her face, obviously. We're not that stupid. Adrienne Archer can scare the meat off your bones just by looking at you. She has reported more kids to the office than all the other safeties put together. She's taller than every one in the fifth grade, including boys and teachers, and she has hands the size of boxing gloves.

Adrienne spun around and glared at me. "Hey, dumbhead, why don't you watch where you're going."

That's how Adrienne talks to people.

"Who are *you* calling dumbhead?" demanded a voice from my pocket.

"What did you say to me?" thundered Adrienne.

"Nothing," I squeaked. "I didn't say a word."

"I'm reporting you, Buzzy Baxter," she said, whipping out her safety notebook.

She began writing my name down.

Jeff edged closer. "He didn't do anything," he protested bravely.

"You're getting reported, Jeff Woodhouse, for mouthing off."

"Mouthing off? I was just making an observation."

"Whose class are you two in?" Adrienne demanded, tapping her pencil against the notebook.

"Mr. Del Duca's."

"Mrs. Ruiz's."

"Aw, lighten up, sweetie-pie."

Doggie dung! That was Nibbles again, poking up from the corner of my pocket, his shiny eyes taking in the whole scene. I jammed my arm against my side and nudged him out of sight with my elbow.

Adrienne's face had turned purple. She bumped her chest against Jeff's. "Don't you tell me to lighten up!"

"I didn't," Jeff squeaked. "I said, uh, brighten up. Like, be happy."

I felt Nibbles scramble through my sweatshirt pocket. His head popped out the other end. "Why don't you pick on someone your own size? If you can find anyone that big."

Why didn't that crazy hamster zip his lips?

Adrienne's eyes darted back to me.

"I didn't say a word," I protested. "My mouth never moved."

Adrienne looked confused. She turned to Cari. "Oh, I get it. You're a vent—vent—one of those people who can talk without moving their lips."

"Ventriloquist," said a helpful voice from my pocket.

"Right," Adrienne snapped. She scowled at Cari. "And you're getting reported too. What's your name?"

"George Washington," snickered Nibbles. I was ready to strangle him.

"Hey! Don't you start getting smart with me." Adrienne glared at Cari.

"Her name is Caridad Perez, and she's in my class," I blurted quickly. If we didn't get out of here fast, the wisecracking hamster was going to get us fried like eggs, sunny side down.

"She's new," Jeff said quickly. "She doesn't know the rules."

"Well, she'd better learn them," snapped Adrienne, scribbling down Cari's name too. "You guys have six seconds to get off the playground, so start moving. One . . . two . . . three . . ."

CHAPTER 10

GOOD GRUB

By the time the word "four" left Adrienne's lips, we were halfway up Franklin Street. Even Cari was keeping up with us. I was surprised how fast she could run in those chunky black boots.

"She's a real meanie!" panted Cari when we finally slowed to a fast walk.

"Yeah, the Hulk clearly lets her safety patrol power go to her head," huffed Jeff.

Nibbles' head popped from my pocket. "Who was that outlaw?" he chuckled.

"Oh, man!" I scolded him. "You have to learn when to keep your mouth shut, Nibbles, especially around Adrienne Archer. She's a safety. Safeties are supposed to help keep the little kids safe on the playground, but instead she scares them to death."

Nibbles clapped his paw over his heart and began to belt out a tune.

Oh, a tale has long been told,
'Bout a girl who's very bold,
But her heart is very cold!
A-a-a-drienne, Adrienne Archer.

I stifled a chuckle and gently nudged the furry fellow down into my pocket. "Cowboy Nibbles. All he needs is a ten-gallon hat and boots, and he'll be famous."

"Well, we'd better get the soon-to-be famous hamster to your house before anything else happens," said Jeff. He jerked a thumb at the street sign on the corner of Center and Franklin. "This is where you turn off, right, Cari?"

"See you tomorrow," I added.

"Wait. I want to come with you," Cari protested. "I want to make sure Nibbles gets to your house safe, too."

"Jeez, won't your mom wonder where you are?"

"She doesn't get home until five. And Jeff is going."

"Jeff always comes to my house after school. His mom teaches second grade at another school, and she picks him up on her way home."

"Can you discuss this later? I'm totally

suffocating in here!" Nibbles' head popped out again. "Let Cari come along," he insisted. "I like her. She gave me that yummy fruit after lunch."

Overruled by a hamster! I didn't want a girl coming over, but I shrugged and gave in.

We walked down Franklin Street to my house. When I opened the front door, Jeff took a deep sniff. "Awesome! Popcorn."

I felt Nibbles wriggling inside my pocket. "What's that yummy smell? Oh, man, that smells delicious. I gotta have some! Let me outta here!"

"Pipe down, Nibbles. We'll get you a snack in a minute, but you have to keep quiet."

We followed the popcorn smell into the kitchen. Grams was chopping vegetables for dinner already. Mom relaxed at the table, sipping a mug of tea. A bag of microwave popcorn sat steaming on the counter.

"How's my favorite grandson?" Grams gave me our secret handshake—palm slap, finger shake, hip wiggle. Jeff had seen it before, but it was a little awkward with Cari there.

"Hi, Buzzy, Jeff."

"Hi, Mom." I waved at Mom's round stomach. "Hello, baby brother."

"Or sister," Mom reminded me and then turned to Cari. I could see her eyebrows lifting a little in surprise that a girl was with us. "Who's this?"

Cari spoke right up. "I'm Caridad Perez. We just moved here this year."

"Her mom's a reporter on WKXR," I added.

"Oh, your mom's Bianca Perez! She does feature stories on the news, right? She did that piece on the corn maze at Angelo's Farm last week. Tell her I thought she did a great job."

"I'll tell her," Cari promised.

"Hi, Buzzy and Jeffy!" My little sister Max came flying into the kitchen and jumped on Jeff. Max was wearing her usual outfit— my old red Power Ranger costume and her cowgirl boots.

Max is a big hugger. I backed away so she wouldn't jump on me and squish Nibbles.

Grams poured the popcorn into a bowl. "How about some apple cider too?" she asked us.

"My bunny wants cider." Max held up Scuzzy, her beat-up bunny. (Real name: Fuzzy. But Max has been dragging him around so long, *Scuzzy* fits him better.)

"We're going to drop off our backpacks in my room," I told Grams. "We'll be back down in a minute."

Jeff and Cari followed me upstairs. I shoved papers out of the way to make a clear spot on my desk for Nibbles.

"So this is your bedroom." Nibbles' nose twitched. "Kind of a slob, aren't you, Buzzy?"

I looked around. Copies of *Kid Power* magazine were stacked beside my unmade bed. Legos and army men were scattered on the floor. An open drawer in my dresser spilled out clothes. Two plates and some cheese-and-cracker wrappers occupied the chair.

Still, it was a little insulting to have a hamster criticize my bedroom. "I wasn't exactly expecting company, wiseguy."

"Speaking of wiseguys, where are we going to put this little troublemaker?" asked Jeff.

Cari picked up a plastic Lego container. "How about this? You're obviously not keeping your Legos in it."

"Perfect." I dumped out a few remaining pieces. "I'll find some paper to line the bottom."

Watching me, Nibbles began to warble again.

Oh give me a home,
And I never will roam
From the darlin' I chose
My sweet Ramblin' Rose.

"What is it with you and country music?"
Jeff demanded.

"I already told you," said Nibbles. "The
manager at Pet Corral always played it in the
store."

I shuffled through old homework papers
in a pile I'd swept to the back of my desk.
"A perfect use for old math homework," I
said with a grin as I ripped several pages in
strips and used them to pad the bottom of
the Lego container. "Okay, Nibbles, your
home is ready." I lowered him in.

Nibbles sniffed around. "Not much of a
view, is there?"

"It doesn't look that comfortable either,"
said Cari. "I'll make you some furniture out of
Lego pieces for now, and we can really fix the
house up later." Cari dropped onto the floor
and scooped up a handful of plastic pieces.

"Okay. And by the way," Nibbles hinted.
"Don't forget: I'm hungry."

"Shocker," said Jeff. "When *aren't* you
hungry?"

"Oh no—we forgot to bring hamster food from school," exclaimed Cari, looking up from snapping together Legos.

Jeff and I glanced at each other. "Pretty dumb," said Jeff.

"We'll have to buy some. We can go tomorrow morning," I said. "It's Saturday. He won't starve in one night."

"I might," said Nibbles, putting his paw on his stomach sadly. "I'm pretty hungry now."

"What else can we feed him?" Cari fussed. "He can't live on popcorn. And we don't want to give him something that could make him sick."

"I don't know," I said. "I don't know what else hamsters eat."

We all stared at each other, worried.

Suddenly Cari spoke into her "microphone." "News flash! We can look online."

"Great idea." I sat at my computer and typed "What do hamsters eat?" Several sites about hamster care appeared. I clicked on the one called *Your Hamster*.

Jeff peered over my shoulder. "*Hamsters love to eat.* No kidding. We knew that already. *Give them fortified pellet mix.* We don't have that."

Cari stood up to see the screen. "*Hamsters will also eat small pieces of most vegetables, such as broccoli, cauliflower, or peas.*"

"Broccoli and cauliflower," I said. "Disgusting." I studied what came next. "*Hamsters also eat carrots.* That's not too bad. We'll give him carrots. Hey, they eat apples too."

Cari laughed. "And hard-boiled eggs. Hamsters like hard-boiled eggs as a treat, and eggs provide important nutrients."

"I don't know if I can get away with boiling an egg," I said. "But I'll try. Okay, let's go get a carrot, an apple, and an egg. That oughta hold him till tomorrow."

"We'll be right back, Nibbles," Cari told him. "We'll bring you some popcorn, too."

"Hurry," Nibbles called. "I'm starving."

Downstairs, Grams put the bowl of popcorn in the center of the table. "Here's your popcorn, guys. Apple cider, coming right up."

Cari and Jeff sat down and began to eat. I got out a small pot and filled it with water. Then I opened the fridge and snagged a baby carrot and a small apple. I shoved both into my pocket. Then I got out an egg.

When I turned around, Grams was frowning at me. "Buzzy, what are you after in the refrigerator?"

"I'm making myself a boiled egg. To go with the popcorn."

"An egg?" said Mom, startled. "I didn't know you liked boiled eggs."

"How can you be hungry enough for all that after the giant lunch I packed?" asked Grams. "And what about the popcorn I just made?"

"I'll eat the egg AND the popcorn, Grams," I promised.

"You'd better eat your dinner too." Grams gestured at the chicken and vegetables she was cutting up for a stir-fry.

"No problem." I put the pot on the burner and turned it on. "How long do I cook this baby?" I asked, holding up the egg.

Grams shook her head. "I'll do it."

I dropped into a seat at the table, glanced at Jeff and Cari, and snagged some popcorn.

"The baby's moving," said Mom. "Want to feel?"

I pressed my palm on her stomach. Something knobby nudged my hand. "Feels like an elbow," I announced. "Or maybe his knee. How you doing, little fella?"

"*He* might be a *she*," Grams and Mom chorused at the same time.

"Doubtful," I said, shoving popcorn into my mouth.

By the time Cari, Jeff, and I had eaten most of the popcorn, the egg was done.

"Thanks, Grams," I said as she handed it to me. I was a little nervous about how long we were taking. I half expected to hear Nibbles shouting at us to hurry it up.

We raced back upstairs to my room and closed the door.

"You took long enough," said Nibbles. "Did you have a party down there?"

"We brought you treats." I fished the carrot and apple out of my pocket and cut off some bits with my scout penknife.

Jeff peeled the egg, and we gave Nibbles slices of that too. Cari gave Nibbles a few pieces of popcorn.

"You're having a feast, Nibbles," Jeff told him.

Nibbles took little bites of everything we gave him. When he tasted the popcorn, he stopped eating and said, "Yummy-yum-yum!

This is delectable. Warm and crunchy."

A cell phone sounded inside Cari's backpack. Cari got it out and looked at it. "Shoot, it's my mom. I forgot to call her." Cari tapped the screen. "*Hola*, Mama. Sorry . . . I forgot to call. . . . No, I'm not home yet, but I'm on my way. . . . Yes, I know it gets dark soon. . . . Yes, I'll do my homework and bring in the trash cans. I love you, too. . . . Bye."

Cari tucked the phone into her backpack and swung it over her shoulder. "I have to go!" She peered into the Lego container. "Bye, Nibbles. I'll come over tomorrow first thing and see how you're doing."

"And don't forget to bring me more treats," said Nibbles.

As Cari ran down the stairs, Jeff poked me. "Who invited her to come back?"

"She doesn't seem to have any problem inviting herself." I looked inside the Lego container. Nibbles was still stuffing his face with popcorn. "We should really be feeding this guy hamster food," I told Jeff. "Mr. D said he shouldn't eat anything else."

Nibbles glanced up at me. "Then how come you bring me Goldfish crackers? Dejon

and Gunner slip me pretzels now and then. And Super Matt gave me apple slices one day. My stomach is used to foreign substances." Nibbles popped another kernel of popcorn into his mouth. "Yummy-yum-yum! What is this stuff called again?"

"Popcorn."

"Ah, yes. Good grub."

CHAPTER 11

NIBBLES GETS LOST

Mom says I could sleep through a four-alarm fire followed by a herd of elephants rampaging through my bedroom. But Saturday morning, a small sound woke me. Someone snuffling back tears. I sat up, blinking sleepily. Max was sitting in the corner in her heart nightgown, her knees tucked up to her chest. She was always the first one awake. No surprise there. But why was she dripping tears onto Scuzzy Bunny?

"Max?" I said, puzzled.

"I didn't mean to do it. Honest, Buzzy. I didn't mean to let your mouse get away."

"WHAT?" I leaped out of bed. The closet door stood open. The Lego box on the closet floor was tipped over and empty.

"I just wanted to play with him," Max said in a wobbly voice. "But he was too fast for me."

"Max!" I grabbed her shoulders. "Nibbles is a hamster, not a mouse. And where is he?"

"He went in there." She pointed to a tiny hole at the bottom of the baseboard.

I got on my hands and knees and stuck my mouth up to the hole. "Nibbles, are you in there?"

No answer. Oh, no. Now what?

I remembered the time we had a problem with mice. Mom saw a mouse run across the kitchen floor. I saw a mouse shoot across the bathroom. Dad found mouse poop in the attic. "These rodents are traveling all over the house," Dad had said. "They must be scrambling around behind the walls." If mice could get around behind the walls, so could Nibbles.

Dad had set a lot of traps to get rid of the mice. What if there was one he'd forgotten somewhere, and Nibbles got caught in it?

I had to find that little guy, and I needed help.

"Max, I'm going to call Jeff. You guard the hole until I come back." At the bedroom door I looked back at Max. "You can't tell Mom and Dad about Nibbles," I whispered. "He's our secret, okay?"

"I promise, Buzzy," said Max solemnly, wiping her eyes on her nightgown.

I opened my bedroom door and peered down the hall to make sure my parents' door was shut. It was. I flew quietly down the stairs into the kitchen, grabbed the phone, and quickly dialed Jeff's house. Unfortunately, Jeff was still asleep. So was his mother.

"Buzz, do you know what time it is?"

"Uh—nine-thirty?" I guessed hopefully.

"Seven o'clock. You woke me at seven a.m. on the only day I can sleep late."

"Sorry," I squeaked.

"I'll get Jeff." Pause. "Who is also asleep, by the way."

A minute later Jeff's groggy voice came on. "Good job waking my mom. Now she'll be grumpy all day."

"It's an emergency, Jeff."

"Everything's an emergency with you."

"No, really. Nibbles is lost."

"You lost Nibbles?" Jeff groaned. "I'm on my way."

I tiptoed quietly back upstairs. "Niblet didn't come out, Buzzy," Max said sadly.

I studied the baseboard. Which way would Nibbles have gone? I pictured him squeezing around wall beams and electric wires. I dropped to my hands and knees and crawled along beside the wall. "Nibbles," I said softly. "Nibbles. Are you in there?" I pressed my ear to the wall. Not a sound.

I circled my whole room, even pulling the bed away from the wall so I could wiggle behind it. Nibbles could have traveled anywhere in the house by now.

I crawled out to the hallway. Every few seconds I bent low and pressed my ear to the wall. When I reached the top of the stairs, I heard the front door open. Jeff stuck his head in.

I waved for him to come in, but as he did, I realized that Cari was behind him. What was she doing here?

They stepped inside. "How could you lose Nibbles?" Jeff demanded.

"Max let him out. She said he scooted into a hole in my bedroom wall."

"Buzzy, what are you guys doing this early?" said Grams, coming through the front door, wearing sweats.

"Oh, hi, Grams. Were you out walking?" I asked.

Grams gave me a suspicious stare. "Just like every morning. What's going on?"

I thought fast. "Uh—we have a science project, and we wanted to start work early."

"Really? Science was always my best subject. Maybe I can help. What's your project about?"

"Electricity," said Cari.

"Bugs," said Jeff. At the exact same time.

"Yeah, well, sort of both," I stammered. "We're studying . . . lightning bugs. We're going to explain what makes them light up."

"Unfortunately, we're not allowed to have help," said Cari politely. "Thanks, though."

"Okay. How about some pancakes? I'll bet you haven't had breakfast yet, and scientists need energy."

"Great," said Jeff. "I love pancakes."

"You love *food*," I whispered as we tiptoed up to my room. Max was still sitting by the floorboard hole.

"He didn't come out, Buzzy," she said sadly.

I pointed. "That's the hole."

Cari was staring at me. "Cute PJ's," she giggled.

Tiger turds! I had forgotten I was in my too-small Spider-Man pajamas that Grams had given me a while ago. I grabbed my jeans off the floor and pulled them over my pajamas.

Cari held up her imaginary microphone and spoke into it. "Coming to you live from Franklin Street, Cari Perez here with breaking news. Nibbles the talking, singing hamster has disappeared. Buzzy Baxter's little sister, Max, took Nibbles out of his Lego box—and the talented hamster vanished."

"Stop announcing that he's lost and let's look for him." I explained about the mice and how they managed to move around our house behind the walls. "I already searched my room. Either Nibbles isn't answering, or he's moved on. I was checking the hall when you guys arrived."

"Even if we locate him, how are you

going to get him out of the wall?" Cari asked.

"Bust a big hole," suggested Jeff, taking a swing with a pretend sledgehammer.

"Brilliant, Jeff. My parents would fry me like bacon," I replied. "Maybe we can talk him back to this little hole by guiding him along the wall with our voices."

"If that doesn't work?" Jeff demanded.

I flung up my hands. "Then, maybe, just maybe, we'll need to make another hole in the wall."

Jeff eagerly rubbed his hands together.

"Let's get moving," said Cari.

"Max, you stay here. Call us if Nibbles comes back," I directed.

"Okay."

"I'll search the hall," volunteered Cari.

"Me and Jeff will take the bathroom," I said. We began crawling around some more, quietly calling, "Nibbles, Nibbles."

I crawled along the bathroom tiles. Jeff crawled after me, and I whispered, "How come you and Cari showed up together? You didn't bring her with you, did you?"

"She was sitting on your front steps when I got here, Buzzy. Said she couldn't wait to see Nibbles again, so she walked over here hoping you'd be up early. She said her mom sleeps late on Saturdays and wouldn't miss her." He spoke into his fist. "Coming to you live from Buzzy Baxter's upstairs bathroom, this is Jumping-Jack Jeff with a late-breaking news flash . . ."

I never heard his news flash. There was a yell of "WHAT THE?" from the hallway, and a scream from Cari. My dad backed into the bathroom and slammed the door. He whirled around, saw me and Jeff, and yelled again.

"You boys scared me to death! What's going on, Buzzy? It's eight o'clock in the morning. There's a strange girl crawling along the hallway, and you boys are hiding in the bathroom!" Dad thrust his hand through his hair. He had serious bed head—his hair stood out like the prickles of a porcupine in defense mode. Now Cari had seen my dad in the boxers that he sleeps in. Great. This day had gone from bad to worse.

"Sorry, Dad." I tried to sell Dad the same lame story we'd told Grams. "They're here to work on a science project on lightning bugs. We're studying them."

"Buzzy, it's October. There are no

lightning bugs around at present, and if there were, they wouldn't be hiding IN OUR BATHROOM."

"Uh, right, Dad, but, uh—remember the lightning bugs me and Jeff caught last summer? I kept them in my bedroom in a jar with air holes in the top. I think some of them escaped. Jeff and me figured they maybe got into the walls and might still be alive."

"Buzz," said Dad, "there are no lightning bugs in our walls, alive or dead. Now, do you think you could search someplace else, and let me use the bathroom in peace?"

"Sure, Dad. No problem. Come on, Jeff." We scuttled back to my room, where Cari was sitting cross-legged on the floor beside Max.

"After my dad goes downstairs," I said, "we can finish searching the upstairs bathroom and hall. Then we'll try the attic."

"Hey, maybe we won't have to search at all." Cari snapped her fingers. "What in the whole world does Nibbles like to eat most?"

Jeff and I looked at each other. "Popcorn!"

"Ding, ding, ding. You are the winners! We can put some popcorn in your room near the hole, and Nibbles will follow the smell."

"Sweet!" I said. "Let's roll. Max, can

you still wait here by the hole in case Nibbles comes back?" Max nodded.

"What's going on up there?" asked Grams as we walked into the kitchen. "I heard shouting."

"Uh, yeah," I stammered. "Dad yelled 'cause we startled him."

Grams nodded. She stood at the stove, a spatula in her hand. "The pancakes are almost ready," she declared.

"We have something we have to do before we eat, Grams."

She waved the spatula. "You can eat first, Buzz."

"Bring on the pancakes," said Jeff.

"Hot off the griddle," she told us, putting a platter on the table. "And some of my special health juice to give you lots of pep." She filled our glasses to the brim.

When she turned back to the griddle, Jeff whispered, "No way!" and slid his glass toward me. "Who knows what effect that stuff will have on humans. I might end up singing cowboy songs all the time."

"That only happened when it mixed with other ingredients," I whispered back.

"Fine. *You* drink it then."

I took a little sip. "Wassa!" I exclaimed, pretending to talk in another language. "Veeloo da massa."

"Yeah, right," said Jeff. "I know you're faking."

Cari took a sip. *"Si,* tastes strange," she whispered. "Makes your tongue tingle."

Grams' pancakes are tasty, even if they are made of healthy whole-wheat flour. Still, it was hard to eat, worrying about poor Nibbles. If anything happened to that popcorn-loving, wisecracking hamster, it would be my fault. I felt sick.

After we finished eating, I got some popcorn out of the plastic container. We hurried quietly upstairs. The bathroom door was closed, and we could hear the shower.

"Max, I have a new job for you," I said. "Can you go down to the kitchen and make sure Grams doesn't come up here? Ask her for some pancakes."

"No!" Max shook her head. "I want to stay here and see if Niblet comes back."

"I know you're worried, but we can't let Grams spot him or he'll be taken away!"

"All right," said Max.

I put handful of popcorn by the hole, and

we sat down to wait. And wait. And wait.

Then from behind the wall came the faint sound of a country tune.

> *O-h-h-h-h, I'm a wandering fool.*
> *Yes, I'm a wandering fool.*
> *And I wander far and near,*
> *Searching for my love,*
> *My Ramblin' Rose.*

"Guess who's back?" Jeff said, grinning.

A minute later a pink nose poked out of the hole.

"Nibbles!" we all shouted.

"You don't have to yell! I'm right here."

"We were afraid you'd get lost forever wandering behind the walls," said Cari dramatically.

"Me too. I got scared when I woke up and my whole house was tipping over. I ran inside this hole in the wall, but I didn't mean to go so far." The nose twitched. "Gross in there. Dried bugs, mouse poop, dust balls." Nibbles sniffed his way forward, then took a deep, appreciative breath. "Ah, popcorn! Yummy-yum-yum!"

CHAPTER 12

PET CORRAL

I was so happy to have Nibbles back, I could have hugged the little guy.

But as we watched him devour the popcorn, a thought struck me. We had to get him some real hamster food. I sighed. Taking care of a hamster was a big responsibility.

"I don't mean to spoil your fun, Nibbles. But we have to get you back on hamster food. All this people food could make you sick."

"How could anything so delicious make me sick?" Nibbles asked.

"You're right, Buzzy," said Jeff. "Let's ride over to Pet Corral and buy some real hamster food."

Nibbles blinked, and his front teeth popped out in a wide grin. "Pet Corral. Yippee!" He danced around in a circle, rear end wagging. "I can't wait to visit my old home."

"No way!" I said sternly. "You attract trouble like a magnet. We are NOT taking you to the store. You can curl up in your comfy Lego box and take a nice, quiet nap while we go get you some food."

Nibbles folded his paws and peered up at us with his golden eyes. "But I want to go, too," he whispered. "Ple-e-ease?"

Cari melted like butter on hot pancakes. "Let him come along. He'll behave. Won't you, Nibbles?"

Jeff and I gave each other a look. Jeff said, "Who said *you're* invited, Cari? Because you're not. Me and Buzzy will handle this."

Cari's cheeks turned pink. "Why can't I come? I helped find Nibbles, didn't I? It was my plan that brought him out of the wall." Cari turned to me.

I shook my head. We'd let her tag after us long enough.

Cari's eyes narrowed. "Spider-Man pajamas," she said quietly.

"What did you say?"

"Who did I see wearing Spider-Man pajamas?" Cari rubbed her forehead like she was thinking. "I can't remember. I just know I saw *someone* crawling around in these cute, little-kid, Spider-Man pajamas. But, if you let me come along, I won't tell anyone."

"That's blackmail!" I protested.

"Well?"

I looked at Jeff, who shrugged. "All right, you can come. Nibbles too. But you"—I pointed at Nibbles—"have to stay in my pocket and keep quiet."

"Quiet as a mouse," said Nibbles. "I mean, quiet as a hamster."

"Him? Quiet?" snorted Jeff. "The hot-shot hamster with the head full of cowboy songs?"

"Don't you like my singing?" Nibbles demanded.

"News flash," Cari said. "Most hamsters can't talk. Remember, Nibbles, if anyone besides us finds out about your special talking talent, they might put you in a circus."

"I'd love to be in a circus." Nibbles struck a pose, puffing out his chest. "Announcing the Daring, Death-Defying Nibbles. What act would I be doing? Trapeze maybe. Or tightrope. Would I get to wear sparkly tights?"

"You wouldn't be in any kind of act, Nibbles," I said. "You'd be in the side show, where they put odd attractions. Bearded ladies. Tattooed men. People who can bend their bodies like a pretzel. And talking hamsters."

"And if a circus doesn't carry you off, scientists may want to experiment on you," said Cari.

"Yeah," said Jeff. "They'd strap you down. Measure you. Poke you. Try to figure out how come you can talk."

"They'd probably make you drink stuff, too," I put in. "Weird chemical stuff to see what effect it has on you."

Nibbles put his paws over his mouth in horror. His eyes were wide and his fur stood on end. "Okay, okay," he mumbled. "I promise to keep quiet."

"You guys wait in the hall while I change." I shoved them out of my room and shut the door. Then I took off my Spidey pajamas and put on jeans and a sweatshirt with a pocket across the front.

I took five dollars from the secret money stash hidden under my socks. *That should be plenty for a bag of seeds*, I thought.

I scooped up Nibbles. "Remember—"

"I know, I know . . . keep quiet!"

I slipped him into my pocket. Downstairs, I found Grams and Max at the kitchen table, eating pancakes and playing Candy Land. Oops! I'd forgotten all about Max. She didn't even know we'd found Nibbles.

Max turned over a card. "Yellow," she said. Then she spotted me and burst out, "Well?"

I smiled and gave her a thumbs up.

"Hooray!" cheered Max.

Grams gave her a funny look. "What are you cheering about?"

Max held up her Candy Land card. "Uh, I love yellow," she told Grams.

I got my bike out, and we pedaled downtown. It was kinda hard to ride with a hamster in my pocket.

We locked our bikes together on the sidewalk outside of Pet Corral. As we pushed through the front door, I could hear country music warbling over the loudspeaker.

Jeff grinned. "Just like Nibbles said."

Nibbles poked his head out. "The old hamster homestead," he said excitedly. "Hear the music, you guys? See my cage! That's where I lived, right over there!"

"Keep quiet, Nibbles," I ordered, pushing him back into my pocket.

We walked toward the back of the store. A man in a fringed cowhide vest and a denim shirt was stacking cans of dog food on a shelf and singing along with the radio. *"My heart is aching, my heart is breaking."*

"That's got to be Cowboy Bob," Cari giggled.

"'Scuse me, mister," Jeff said.

"Hey, pardners. How can I help you?"

"We need hamster food," I said.

"For our hamster. Our ordinary hamster," Jeff said nervously. "He doesn't do any tricks. Except run on his wheel, but all hamsters do that."

Cowboy Bob chuckled. "I reckon I can find some ordinary food for an ordinary hamster."

We followed him along the aisle, past dog toys and collars. I kept my hand over the lump that was Nibbles in my pocket. I could feel him quivering with eagerness. "Right there, pardners. Gourmet Blend and Regular. Bring it up front when you're ready. If you have any questions give me a shout."

I read the prices marked on the shelf. "Huh! Gourmet Blend comes in a smaller bag and costs two bucks more than regular! Not much choice there."

I reached for the bag of regular hamster

food. Nibbles' head popped out of my pocket. "Put that back. If I've gotta eat seeds, I want the gourmet ones."

"Nibbles, you're not being quiet."

I took down the regular hamster food. Nibbles saw it.

"No way," he yelled. "I want the gourmet seeds! Cowboy Bob . . . !"

"Nibbles! You promised to keep quiet!" I stuffed him deep into my pocket and grabbed the gourmet bag of food.

"Did you call?" asked Cowboy Bob. He was coming toward us.

"Yes. No. I mean, we're ready." I held out the bag. "We're going to buy the gourmet food. Nothing but the best for our sweet little hamster."

"I thought you'd see it my way," piped a voice from my pocket.

CHAPTER 13

YUMMY YUMMY CHURROS

Out on the sidewalk, we grabbed our bikes. Before we even pushed off, Cari's backpack started beeping. She fished out her cell phone and read the text message. "Uh oh! My mom is asking where I am."

"I thought you said she slept late."

"Apparently, not this late," Cari retorted, tapping out a message. "It stinks being an only child. She worries about me too much." She looked at Jeff and me hopefully. "Can you stop at my house and explain where we were? She might not be so mad."

"Where we were? Uh, at a pet store buying food for a kidnapped talking hamster. *That's* going to help?"

"Ple-e-ease," Cari pleaded.

"I can't," Jeff shrugged. "I'm supposed to be helping my dad clean the basement today. He's probably already called Buzzy's house looking for me."

"All right, all right—I'll ride to your house with you, Cari. But I've got to leave right away. I have to hustle home and do some serious work on my Me Museum."

We got on our bikes and started pedaling.

"You're still not finished with that thing?" Cari asked in disbelief. "You go on Wednesday, right?"

"Yes, right." I swung the bag of hamster food. "Here's the problem. I have nothing exciting to include in my autobiography. I don't have a mom who's a TV news reporter."

Cari shook her head a little. "Yeah, but I can't help what my mom does for a living."

"It's still exciting. And I've never gone bungee jumping like Dejon or had a bear get into my tent on a camping trip. My family has never even taken a camping trip."

"So what? The Me Museum doesn't have to be exciting. Most of the kids just talked about their sports and stuff. Just write about your ordinary life."

Up ahead the traffic light turned red, and we coasted to a stop. Cari turned left into a development of brick townhouses. In this neighborhood, none of the houses had yards.

"It's like this," I sighed, hunching my shoulders. "I've always been known for being funny. Kids expect me to put on some hilarious presentation. But I don't have anything funny or crazy this time. I'm gonna be standing up there like a big dork, unless I find something to kick it up a notch."

"I have the perfect solution! Wear your Spidey jammies for your presentation. That would be hilarious."

I glared at her. "I thought you were going to keep quiet about that."

"Sorry, Buzzy." She put her fingers over her mouth, trying not to giggle. "I won't mention it again. And I'll try to think of something to help with your Me Museum."

When we got to Cari's house, her mom was watching for us. She opened the door wearing fancy jeans and a black sweater. Long silver earrings dangled from her ears. My mom wears sweats on the weekend.

"Caridad Perez! *Mi pequena*. Where were you?" She hugged Cari and scolded her at the same time. "I was so worried. When I woke up, your bed was empty. I had no idea where you were. I thought you might be kidnapped."

"Mo-o-om! Stop being so dramatic. You know I wasn't kidnapped. I went to Buzzy's house to work on a project. I didn't want to wake you up."

Cari's mom looked over Cari's shoulder at me.

I gave a little wave. "Hi, I'm Buzzy."

"*Hola,* Buzzy. Welcome to our home. Would you like some Mexican hot chocolate? I could heat up *churros* too."

Cari's Mom smiled, like she does on TV. I expected her to say, "It's *Coffee Bites with Bianca,*" like on her show. Ever since my mom met Cari, we've been watching the news every morning so we can see Bianca do her *Coffee Bites* news segments as we eat breakfast.

"Mom's churros are delicious!" Cari told me.

I would have loved some hot chocolate and churros. But I really did need to go home and work on the stupid Me Museum. Besides, I wasn't sure how long Mr. Chatty was going to keep quiet. If I let Mrs. Perez give me hot chocolate, chances were, he'd come leaping out of my pocket and demand a snack, too.

"I'd better get going," I said reluctantly. "I have to work on another project for school."

"Take a churro to go, then," said Mrs. Perez. She left the room and came right back with a paper towel wrapped around something. It was warm and smelled delicious.

Cari walked me to the door. "Sorry, about my mom," she whispered. "She's a little dramatic."

"She's really nice," I said.

I ran down Cari's steps and picked up my bike. As I pedaled along the sidewalk, I bent my head and said to Nibbles, "Great job keeping quiet, Nibbles."

"I'm suffocating in here!" he mumbled. "And hungry. Get me home so I can have some food."

"Here, you can have a tiny bite of this churro. It's delicious." It was chewy and cinnamony and sweet.

I broke off a tiny piece and stuck it in my pocket.

"Yummy-yum-yum!"

GET ME OUT!

When I got home, I didn't see anyone. I dumped my bike on the grass and pulled the front door open. I could hear Grams and Mom talking in the kitchen. No sign of Dad or Max. I darted up the stairs to my room and shut the door.

I poured gourmet pet food into the jar lid I was using as a food dish for Nibbles. Nibbles sniffed at the seeds. Then he sampled a few, chewing thoughtfully. He reminded me of those food experts you see on TV. Finally he patted his stomach.

"Ahh," he muttered approvingly. "Good grub."

When he finished eating, his cheeks bulged with extra seeds he'd tucked away for later. "Now, time for a nap." I watched him burrow under the torn-up newspaper.

"Buzzy, lunchtime," called Grams.

"I'm going to go eat lunch," I told Nibbles. "Be quiet while I'm gone."

"Gotcha, Pardner," came his sleepy voice.

I hurried downstairs, pretty hungry myself. Dad, Mom, and Max were already at the kitchen table. I grabbed a chair and joined them. Grams had made turkey wraps. I grabbed one from the platter and took a big bite. I tried to peek and see what was in it.

"Hummus," Grams told me. "And roasted peppers."

"I'm starving," I said.

"Me too," said Dad. "Painting's hard work." Aqua-colored paint had spattered his clothes and speckled his hair. He'd been painting the room that was being turned from his office into the baby's bedroom. Eventually, either me or Max would have to share our room—depending on whether the baby was a boy or girl. Already, Max was sharing her room with Grams, who slept in Max's other twin bed.

"I have to go to Home Depot after lunch," Dad said, crunching on a pickle.

"You need to be back by one," Grams reminded him. "I'm taking Bonnie to her doctor's appointment. And Max will be here by herself."

"Excuse me?" I stared from Grams to Dad. "I'm here."

"I can drive myself to the doctor," Mom protested.

"No driving," Grams said sternly. "That's what the doctor said last visit."

"If I'm not back right on time, Buzzy can watch Max for a few minutes," Dad suggested.

"Do you think he's responsible enough?" asked Mom.

"What do you think I'm going to do?" I retorted indignantly. "Light the gas stove and set the house on fire? Or lock Max in the closet?" Oops, that wasn't the greatest example to give since that time I'd locked Dad's keys in the car.

"I think he can handle it," said Dad.

"All right." Mom nodded reluctantly. "Buzzy, you need to work on your Me Museum."

"Don't remind me," I groaned. This Me Museum was ruining my life.

I sneaked a slimy strip of roasted pepper left from my wrap and carried it upstairs for

Nibbles. He was still curled up under the shavings, so I sat down at my desk and pulled my notebook out of my backpack. I flipped it open and stared at the couple of pathetic, measly sentences that were all I had written so far for my autobiography. I chewed on my pencil, doodled some aliens, and gave a huge sigh.

"What's wrong, pardner?"

I peeked into Nibbles' house. "I thought you were sleeping."

"Who can sleep with all that groaning?"

"Sorry. Here, I brought you a snack." While Nibbles munched on the pepper, I explained about the stupid Me Museum I was working on. "You were there when Lindsey presented her Me Museum. Remember? You got me in major trouble with the comments you kept making."

"Oh, yes, Lindsey. She's the one who showed off the little shoes and the gigantic socks."

"That's the girl." I turned the paper over so I wouldn't see all that empty white space waiting for me to fill out. "I don't feel like working. How about if I build a maze, and you can try to find your way to the center?"

"Sounds like a plan, pardner."

I lifted Nibbles out of the Lego box. Then I pulled the bin of blocks from the back of my closet and started laying them out on the floor. I used to love doing mazes when I was little. You always heard about scientists experimenting with rats finding their way through mazes. I wondered how a hamster would do.

"Buzzy?" Grams stuck her head in my door.

I froze, hoping she wouldn't see Nibbles crouching behind a block. "Yeah, Grams."

"Your Mom and I are leaving. Max is in her room playing princess. You're in charge until your dad gets home."

"I can handle that, Grams." I heard her go down the stairs. "Coast is clear, Nibbles. And I'm just about finished. Another block here, a couple there . . . Okay. Let's see you find your way through this."

"What's my prize?" demanded Nibbles.

"What prize?"

"When I find my way to the middle, I need a prize. I hope it's food," he hinted.

"Man, you're unbelievable. All right." I hunted through my messy desk and found half a stale pretzel stick. "This good?"

"Okay," he agreed. Nibbles raced into the opening and scurried through the maze.

"Hey, no fair peeking over the wall," I complained.

"Who needs to peek? I could have found my way blindfolded." He quickly reached the center and did a little victory song and dance holding his pretzel up like a trophy. Then he took a bite. "Mmm. Not as good as popcorn, but still tasty."

NIBBLES AND THE CRAZY SCIENCE EXPERIMENT **117**

Over his munching, I heard another sound. Max was calling "Buzzy!" in a quavery voice.

I ran into the hall. The bathroom door was shut.

"Max, are you in there?" I knocked and then tried to open the door, but it was locked from the inside. "Max, open up!"

"I can't," Max said. "It's stuck."

"You know we're not supposed to lock this door. Dad told us a jillion times this lock jams up."

"I didn't mean to lock it," Max retorted. "I just turned that metal thing."

Toad turds! This was not good news.

"Max," I pressed my face to the door. "Try again. Turn that metal thing back the other way."

I heard a raspy jiggle. "It won't turn, Buzzy." Max sounded mad. "Get me out!" She banged on the door.

Great! Mom and Grams hadn't been gone ten minutes, and Max had locked herself in the bathroom.

I rattled the door handle. "Max, try again. MAX!" I kicked the door in frustration.

"Whoa, pardner." Nibbles had come into

the hall, looking up at me with his shiny eyes. "You're acting as crazy as popcorn on a hot skillet."

"Max is locked in the bathroom," I told him. "If Dad comes home and finds her stuck in there crying, they won't trust me again till I'm twenty, after my stupid joke about locking her in the closet. My mom always says I need to be more responsible."

Nibbles sat back on his haunches. His whiskers twitched as he thought. "This calls for drastic measures!" He flexed his muscles. "Super Hamster! I'll have to rescue her myself."

"Nibbles, the door's locked. How are you gonna get in?"

"Remember when I was lost inside the wall?" he said. "Well, at one point I found an opening. I came out in the bathroom."

"Can you find your way there again?" I asked doubtfully.

"I'll try." Nibbles rubbed his front paws together and gave me a sideways glance. "Why don't you get some sustenance for me."

"Sustenance?"

"Food, Buzzy. What about those little Goldfish crackers you used to feed me.

They're *so* tasty." His nose twitched in anticipation.

I couldn't believe this little guy. "We're having a crisis, and you're thinking about food!"

"I'm weak with hunger," he told me. "Do you want me to faint in the middle of my rescue mission?"

"You just ate a pretzel. Oh, all right. You get going. I'll get the Goldfish. And remember, not a word. Max doesn't know you can talk."

Nibbles scurried off to my room. I charged down to the kitchen and grabbed a few Goldfish. I climbed the stairs two at a time.

Max was still crying. Louder. Harder.

I slumped down with my back against the door and waited.

Then I heard a beautiful sound—laughter. From inside the bathroom. "Buzzy, guess who just popped out of a hole in the wall?"

"Who, Max?"

"Niblet."

"It's *Nibbles*. And that's great, Max. Now you don't have to be scared anymore. Nibbles will keep you company." I had another idea now that she had calmed down. "I'll get some of your favorite books and read them to you from out here."

"Okay," she agreed.

I ran into her room and grabbed a few books off the shelf. I picked up Scuzzy Bunny, too. I sat back down outside the bathroom door, realizing I was weak with relief.

"Okay, Max, I've got a few books to read you. And I brought Scuzzy Bunny. He'll sit out here with me, and Nibbles will keep you company."

I flipped open a book and started to read.

And that's where we were when Dad got home.

"Dad," I yelled. "We're up here. Max locked herself in the bathroom."

"Uh-oh. Hold on—I'll get my toolbox."

While Dad tinkered with the lock, I told him what had happened. "Max wouldn't stop crying, but I calmed her down by reading to her and holding Scuzzy Bunny right here."

The lock popped open, and Dad turned the knob. Max stood there in her princess gown. Sweaty and tear-streaked. I saw Nibbles disappear behind the toilet.

Dad swung Max up in his arms. "Hey, princess, did you lock yourself in your tower?"

"I did." Max giggled. "And Niblet rescued me."

I held my breath, but Dad either hadn't heard Max or thought she was talking nonsense.

"Buzz!" Dad ruffled my hair. "I'm proud of you. You stayed calm and showed good thinking reading to her and comforting her."

"Thanks, Dad."

Dad and Max went downstairs, while I grabbed Nibbles and hurried back into my room.

"You saved the day, Nibbles," I said as I put him down. "You're a hero."

"I guess I am." He puffed himself up and took a little bow. His gold fur practically glowed. "Too bad Cari's mom can't do a little story about me for the news." He whipped out an invisible microphone. "News flash: It's time for my crackers!"

CHAPTER 15

THE STUBBORN HAMSTER

Nibbles had a great weekend. So great, in fact, he didn't want to go back to school on Monday morning.

"Why should I?" Nibbles was reclining in the Lego chair Cari had built for him. Max had added a sock stuffed with cotton balls for a pillow. Nibbles' room looked like a Hollywood movie set. "Here I can run around. Eat popcorn. Watch movies with Max. We were going to watch *Toy Story* today."

"You and Max already watched that."

"I want to see it again. It's hilarious."

"Hold on . . ." I shot him a suspicious look. "Does Max know you can talk?"

"No." Nibbles flipped a sunflower seed in the air and caught it in his mouth. "She talks to me. I don't talk to her."

"Come on, Nibbles. You have to go back to school. I don't have time to argue. Jeff is already downstairs waiting for me."

"Should've thought ahead before you hamster-napped me, pardner." Nibbles chuckled. "You should've considered that I might not want to go back."

I stared down at him. Steam was practically coming out of my ears. How do you handle an uncooperative hamster?

"I'll make a deal with you," I told him. "If you go to school without a fuss, I'll bring you popcorn every day. And next weekend, I'll sneak you home again."

I watched Nibbles think it over, whiskers quivering. I knew he couldn't turn down all that popcorn. "Okay," he agreed. "Deal."

That was one problem solved. But another was waiting for me at school: How was I going to get Nibbles past Adrienne Archer and Mr. Del Duca?

I heard someone knock on the front door. Couldn't be Jeff—he was already here. It had to be Cari. I knew she couldn't stay away. I reached for Nibbles.

"Whoa!" he protested. "Where's my popcorn?"

"That starts tomorrow, Nibbles. You've been stuffing your face all weekend."

"Oh, no you don't! Hand over some popcorn now, or I'm not budging."

"Alright, alright! I'll go downstairs and pop some," I snapped. "Now, get in my pocket!" I scooped Nibbles up and thrust him into the front of my sweatshirt. I was beginning to feel like a kangaroo carrying a baby around in her pouch every day.

In the kitchen, Grams was cracking eggs into a bowl. "Morning, Buzzy. Your eggs will be ready in a minute."

Jeff was hunched over the kitchen table, pushing scrambled eggs onto his fork with a piece of toast. He motioned to his plate. "Want half? This was supposed to be yours."

Cari sat across from him wearing a hot pink headband and with her backpack slung over the chair.

"Don't worry about me," I said sarcastically. "I just live here."

"Jeff said he didn't eat much breakfast at home," Grams explained. "I knew you wouldn't mind, Buzzy. This next batch will be ready in a jiffy."

I shot a look at Cari. She was sipping a

glass of O.J.

"What—do you live here now, too?"

"I had my mom drop me off. I thought it would be nice to walk to school with you guys. We can talk about our 'science project.'"

"I thought we finished the science project," I retorted.

Grams was busy at the stove, stirring my eggs around in the frying pan.

Trying not to attract attention, I edged toward the snack cabinet, fished out a bag of microwave popcorn, and slid it into the microwave.

"So, Buzzy . . ." Cari raised her eyebrows. "Do you have . . . ?"

I nodded and patted my pocket. "He didn't want to go," I whispered. "I had to bribe him with popcorn." I jerked my head at the microwave where the bag was beginning to puff up.

"Man, that little guy eats more than I do," Jeff observed.

"Nobody eats more than you, Jeff." *Oh no!* That was my pocket talking.

"Quiet down," I muttered. Dopey hamster was going to get us snagged by Grams.

Max stormed into the kitchen, wearing

her princess nightgown. "Where is he?" she demanded.

Cari, Jeff, and I snapped to attention. I put a finger to my lips and pointed at Grams.

Max came closer. "Where's Niblet, Buzzy?" she asked softly.

"His name is Nibbles." I patted my pocket. "He's right here. He has to go back to school this morning, Max."

"NO!" She stamped her bare foot. "I want to play with him. I'm going to make him a Halloween costume." Max turned to Cari. "I made Niblet a sock pillow to go with his chair."

"I'll bet it's cute," said Cari. Max smiled.

Grams turned around, holding the pan of eggs. "Hand me a plate, will you, Buzzy. Max, do you want some scrambled eggs?"

"Actually, Grams," I interrupted, "I think I'll have breakfast-to-go this morning. You can give my eggs to Max." I grabbed a blueberry pastry from the cupboard and slung my backpack over my shoulder.

"That's not a healthy start to your day," Grams protested. "You need protein—" Grams took a deep sniff. "Do I smell popcorn?"

"Popcorn?"—*ding!* went the timer— "Oh, you mean this?" I opened the microwave door and grabbed the steaming bag. "I need to bring popcorn to school today for, uh . . ."

"Our science project," Cari offered.

"Yeah, our science project."

Grams looked puzzled. "Why do you need popcorn for a project on electricity?"

"Well, uh, electricity powers the microwave, and the microwave popped the popcorn." I added, "Like I said, Max can have my scrambled eggs."

"I don't want your eggs," hissed Max fiercely. "I want Niblet."

"Nibbles!"

"Whatever." Max stamped her foot again. "I want him to stay here."

"We have to get him back to school," I whispered at Max.

Grams was staring at us like we were crazy.

"Let's get going." I jerked my chin at Cari and Jeff and bolted for the door—bumping right into my mom.

Hopping hamsters! Could this day get any crazier?

"Hi, Mom. Late for school." I tried to

squeeze past. Not easy to do with her bulging baby-belly filling up the doorway.

"Owww!" Uh-oh. Nibbles was getting squashed.

"Sorry, Buzzy," Mom apologized.

"No problem." I stood back to let her pass. "We're outta here." I flashed my pearlies at Mom and patted her stomach. "Bye, little brother." I headed for the door with Jeff and Cari right behind.

Outside we hurried along the sidewalk. "Omigosh, what a nightmare," I said.

"Where's my popcorn?" Nibbles' head popped out of my pocket.

I stopped and tore open the bag. Steam poured out. "Not a healthy breakfast, Nibbles," I reminded him.

"Look who's talking, Mr. Pastry."

Jeff stuck out a hand. "Hit me up with some of that popcorn."

I spilled popcorn into Jeff's hand and dumped some into my pocket. "There you go, Nibs, your in-flight meal. That's all you get, Jeff. This bag has to last all day."

"Yeah, lay off my popcorn, Jeff," Nibbles called and then began munching. "Mmm, yummy-yum-yum."

"We need to hurry," Cari reminded us, "if we want to sneak him inside before the bell rings."

We broke into a slow run. "Earthquake!" yelled Nibbles. "Take it easy, will you?"

"Tell that crazy hamster to be quiet," panted Jeff.

Nibbles stuck his head out. "You wouldn't be quiet if you were getting thrown around like this."

When we reached school, kids were already hanging out on the playground. Dejon, Super Matt, and Gunner were playing four square. "Hey, guys, come play with us," Dejon called, bouncing the ball.

"Can't right now. Got something we have to do." I kept moving, stepping as gently as I could so I wouldn't jostle Nibbles and start him yelling again. In fact, I concentrated so hard on walking without upsetting the hamster that I didn't pay attention to what was right in front of me. A bright green safety belt, worn by the Hulk herself!

CHAPTER 16

RETURN OF THE HULK

"**W**here do you think *you're* going?" Adrienne Archer demanded.

I fished for an answer and came up empty. "Uh . . . uh . . . uh."

"Mr. Del Duca said we could come in early to take our science project up to the classroom," Cari said quickly.

Adrienne looked at us suspiciously. "I don't see any science project."

Cari dug around in her backpack. She held up a plastic baggie so Adrienne could see it. "We raised pollywink bugs. They change color to match the background. Camouflage, you know. Do you see them?"

"No!" Adrienne leaned close, squinting. "I don't see anything."

"Maybe you need glasses," piped a voice from my pocket.

Adrienne gave me a slit-eyed look. "What did you say?"

"Bad eyes and big feet, too. What size are those boats you're wearing? Your feet are bigger than Lawrence Clayburn's."

That hamster was going to get me beat up!

Adrienne pushed her face up close to mine. "You are in big trouble, Buzzy Baxter."

I believed her. I was shaking. She'd report me again, and I'd get detention. Mr. D would yell at me for getting reported on Friday and again on Monday. Worst of all, Adrienne would be out to get me for the rest of the year.

I could feel kids crowding around us, waiting to see Adrienne chop me into fish bait.

"Why don't you pick on someone your own size?" came from my pocket again.

"What did Buzzy say?" someone asked behind me.

"He said, 'Pick on someone your own size.'"

"Whoa, he's got guts talking back to Adrienne Archer."

Adrienne's face had turned the color of a ripe tomato. "I'll squash you into mush, Buzzy Baxter," she snarled.

"Oh yeah? You and what army?"

"Shut up," I yelled to Nibbles.

"What?" said the Hulk. "Don't you tell me to shut up."

"You tell her, Buzzy!"

"Way to go, Buzzy!"

Adrienne looked around. So did I. A bunch of kids were now crowded around us, watching. And every kid was glaring at her.

The Hulk just stood there looking confused. Nobody ever stood up to her. But I knew what to do. This was our chance. "Let's go," I hissed to Cari and Jeff.

We squirmed through the crowd and darted inside.

"Earthquake!" squealed Nibbles as I raced up the stairs to the second floor. At the top, I paused and held my pocket wide. Nibbles lay on his back, eyes closed, popcorn scattered all over him. "Am I dead?" he panted.

"No, you're not dead, Nibbles! But you almost got *me* killed back there."

"I'm sorry. I truly am." He gave a weak twitch and sat up. "But seriously, have you noticed the size of her feet?"

"I can't believe you stood up to Adrienne Archer, Buzzy," exclaimed Jeff.

"Not me. Nibbles took her on."

"*Si*, he's the bravest little hamster in the west," said Cari, laughing. "He should be on the news."

"Good thinking about those 'bugs,'" I told Cari.

"It was the bag of pretzels from my lunch, which I dumped. Now I have crushed pretzels all over my backpack."

We hurried down the hallway and stopped outside our classroom.

I took a quick peek inside. Mr. D wasn't at his desk. Sweet. Maybe he went to get coffee. We could slip Nibbles into his cage before the bell rang.

"Come on," I said, darting toward the science table.

"Hey, you guys."

I spun around, startled. *Rat poop!* Mr. D was there after all, writing the homework assignment on the whiteboard along the side wall. "What are you three doing inside the building before the bell again? Did you miss school so much you couldn't wait to hurry back this morning?"

"I, uh, I . . . yeah, we did," I mumbled. "You know us. We love school."

R-R-R-I-I-I-N-N-G-G! The bell saved us from any more of Mr. D's questions. But now it was too late to sneak Nibbles back into his cage. Footsteps rumbled along the first floor and thudded up the steps. Kids came flooding into the classroom.

"Hey, Baxter, way to take down the Hulk on the playground!" called Dejon. Super Matt slapped me on the back. "You're better than Superman," he laughed.

"Okay, team, keep it down," called Mr. D. "Unpack your things and take your seats. Jeff, you seem to be having a problem these days remembering which class you belong in."

"Who me? I was just leaving." Jeff backed out, giving me worried glances the whole time.

Cari and I sat down at our desks, me with a warm hamster still curled up in my pocket.

"Who's our leader for morning exercises?" Mr. D asked.

Amaya waved her hand and walked up front. "Everyone stand for the Pledge of Allegiance."

"Psst . . . Buzzy." Mei-Lin pushed a folded piece of paper at me. When I opened it, the words BUZZY THE BRAVE stared out. All caps, with a wreath of hearts around the edge.

Everyone—including Mei-Lin, apparently—thought I was a big hero for standing up to Adrienne. I looked up and she gave me a little smile. *Donkey dung!*

After the pledge came "The Star-Spangled Banner."

"O-oh say can you see . . ." Guess who joined in on the next line? *"By the dawn's early light . . ."*

Mei-Lin gave me a puzzled look. Could she hear a voice coming from my pocket? I sang louder to drown Nibbles out. *"WHAT SO PROUDLY WE HAILED . . ."*

The voice coming from my pocket got louder too. *"AT THE TWILIGHT'S LAST GLEAMING . . ."*

I sang so loud I thought my lungs would burst. ***"WHOSE BROAD STRIPES AND BRIGHT STARS . . ."***

By the time we finished, the whole class was grinning in my direction. "Well," said Mr. D, shaking his head, "somebody's feeling extra patriotic this morning." He opened his planner. "Okay, team, take out your homework."

I slumped down in my seat. The day was just beginning, and I was already exhausted. Plus, I still had to figure out how to smuggle Nibbles back into his cage.

Super Matt came ambling to the back of the room to sharpen his pencil. He stopped at the science table. "Hey, Nibbles, how's it going, buddy?" *Uh-oh.* I felt the hairs on the back of my neck stand up. Matt leaned closer to the cage, frowning. "Mr. Del Duca, I don't see Nibbles in here!"

"He's probably asleep under the shavings," said Mr. D, walking toward the science table.

Everyone turned to look at Super Matt. Even Cari. I slouched lower in my seat, panic flooding over me. Now what?

"No, he's not. And the cage isn't locked. Nibbles is gone!"

"Maybe Mr. Pete knocked the latch loose when he was cleaning," said Amaya.

"Then Nibbles escaped from the cage and jumped down from the table," Dejon added.

"Poor Nibbles!" said Mei-Lin. "Once he got down, he couldn't get back up. That means he's had nothing to eat all weekend."

No food all weekend? Just gourmet seeds, hard-boiled egg, slices of apple, and popcorn galore. I almost choked as I pictured Nibbles right now, munching away in my pocket.

"How long can a hamster live without food?" asked Lindsey, her eyes wide. Nobody answered.

"Let's not panic, gang," said Mr. D. "He's probably still in the classroom. Watch where you step while we search for him."

Kids began crawling along the aisles between the desks, calling, "Here, Nibbles!"

This was ridiculous. A whole class of kids down on their hands and knees searching, while Nibbles was safe in my pocket. Mei-Lin knelt by the bookcase and began pulling books out to look behind them. Amaya looked in the coffee mug on Mr. D's desk—like Nibbles could climb up on the desk in the first place.

I slid off my seat and pretended to look, too. I felt like an idiot, calling, "Nibbles," when he was in my pocket the whole time.

I'd better warn him, I thought. "Nibbles! You hear what's going on?"

A whispered yes came from my pocket.

"For Pete's sake, keep your trap shut till . . ."

Nibbles' head popped out. "Isn't it exciting? Everybody searching for me."

"Shhh."

Cari wriggled alongside me. "Let him out," she said out of the corner of her mouth. "I'll pretend to find him."

I nodded, and we headed for the front of the room. Hidden behind Mr. D's desk, I slipped Nibbles out of my pocket and backed away.

"I found him," Cari yelled. "I found Nibbles!" She stood up, hands cupped,

Nibbles' head peeking out.

"Good girl, Caridad!" exclaimed Mr. Del Duca.

"Yay, Cari," cheered Mei-Lin and Lindsey.

"After you put him back, you can help yourself to an Awesome Treat," said Mr. D. He looked puzzled. "I thought I searched around my desk."

Cari set Nibbles inside the cage and latched the door. Everyone crowded around to see.

"I'm so glad he's safe. I'd die if anything happened to that little guy," sighed Amaya.

"Nothing to eat or drink for three days," added Lindsey. "Poor thing must be starving."

The kids watched Nibbles. "That's strange," Matt said slowly. "He's not going near his food."

Dejon picked up the magnifying glass on the science table and peered at Nibbles through it. "I wonder what's wrong with him," he said.

I heard a snicker of laughter. I glared at Cari, warning her not to give us away. But Cari was sending me the same stern look I was giving her.

We both looked at Nibbles, hunched down in the wood shavings. His eyes were closed, and he was quivering all over.

"Poor little hamster!" cooed Amaya. "He's too frightened to eat."

Frightened? Nibbles wasn't frightened. He wasn't hungry either, after his non-stop weekend feast. No—he was trying not to laugh!

"Can I give him a treat?" begged Shawnda.

"That's a good idea," said Mr. D. "Poor little guy does seem a little shaken up."

Shawnda went to her desk and took out her lunch. She came back with a small carrot. "Can I give him this?"

"Sure, a small piece of it," said Mr. D. After Shawnda had slid the carrot bit into Nibbles' bowl, Mr. D clapped his hands and said, "Okay, everybody, back to your desks. Let's give Nibbles some quiet time."

I wished Nibbles would give *me* some quiet time. Keeping that little guy under control was wearing me to a frazzle.

CHAPTER 17

CANDY CORN MATH

I slumped down at my desk, buried in problems. How was I going to keep that hamster out of trouble for the rest of the year if I couldn't even keep him quiet for one day?

Another thing: Even if we kept Nibbles a secret till school ended, what then? Would he secretly have to live at my house all summer?

And if all that wasn't enough, I had one more problem. My Me Museum was due in two days, and I still had nothing to present.

"Okay, gang, Halloween is on the way, so we're going to play some trick-or-treat math." Mr. Del Duca whipped open a desk drawer and held up a jar of candy corn. Then he set five paper cups on his desk and began filling them with candy. "For three weeks, we've been working on fractions, so you're ready for a quick drill. I'll read five fraction problems," he continued. "The first one to solve all five correctly wins a cup of candy corn."

"Great! I'm starving."

Oh no! I smacked my forehead. I thought Nibbles was sleeping. Instead, he was standing up, front paws against the bars.

"First problem," said Mr. D. "Find four-fifths of twenty." We all scribbled that down.

"Sixteen," hissed Nibbles.

Without thinking, I wrote sixteen.

Nibbles is working these problems out in his head? I thought. *The hamster's a math genius!*

Mr. D continued reading the next four problems. Nibbles whispered and I wrote down the answers for each.

"Ready!" Nibbles shouted.

Mr. D looked up. "Was that you, Buzzy?"

"Uh, no. I mean yes." What else could I say? I read out Nibbles' answers.

"Whoa!" Mr. D took a step back, hands up. "I'm impressed. That was fast. Okay, come get your cup of candy corn."

My heart was thumping loudly. Had anyone noticed Nibbles giving me the answers? I hurried up to Mr. Del Duca's desk to collect my candy corn.

Nibbles was watching when I sat back down. I flipped a few pieces of candy corn into his cage.

"That's not half," he objected. "You need to split it evenly with me."

Are you kidding me?! I thought. But I didn't have time to argue so I tossed a few more pieces his direction.

"Okay, math wizards. Next problem: Find three-fourths of thirty-two." Mr. D continued reading the rest of the problems.

"That's 24," came Nibbles' whisper.

I shook my head. I wasn't going to be the first one done the five problems this time. Let someone else win the candy corn.

"Yes it is. Trust me. 24. **24**. **24!**"

"Okay, I'm writing it down. Look, see." I said, scribbling the answer on my paper.

"Buzzy, work quietly back there," said Mr. D.

The hamster kept feeding me answers. Pretty soon I'd won my second cup of candy.

"No fair," grumbled Dejon. "Buzzy already won."

"Good job, Buzzy," Mr. D said, looking puzzled. "You're on a math roll today."

I rushed up to get my candy corn. Mr. D

was giving me a look, like he knew something was going on but couldn't quite figure out what.

This time I put the candy corn in my desk right away to head off an argument with the furry math fiend. "I'll give you more later. If you eat too much, it'll make you sick."

"No fair," protested Nibbles.

"I can't take it anymore!" I yelled, throwing my pencil into the air.

"Buzz, relax." Mr. D held his hand up. "It's just a game. And you won anyway."

"Sorry." I shoved my hand through my hair, breathing hard. "I'm a little stressed out today."

"I can tell," said Mr. D. "You keep talking to yourself."

I caught Cari's eye and motioned to the door. Then I raised my hand.

"Yes, Buzzy?"

"Uh, bathroom," I said through clenched teeth, trying to make it sound like an emergency.

Mr. D nodded. "Don't forget the hall pass," he said.

As I scuttled toward the door, Cari coughed. "Can I get a drink, Mr. D? There's something caught in my throat."

"Go ahead," said Mr. D, but now I could see him giving us suspicious looks.

In the hall, Cari headed straight for the water fountain. "Good one!" I told her.

Cari gulped some water. "Thanks. Now, what's going on?"

"Let me get Jeff first." The door to Mrs. Ruiz's classroom was open. I waited until her back was turned and motioned to Jeff.

Jeff came into the hall, swinging the bathroom pass. "What's up?"

"That hamster is making me CRAZY! I can't take it anymore! He keeps singing, calling out, making wisecracks. Just now he was feeding me answers in math."

"That was Nibbles?" said Cari, wide-eyed.

"I didn't know hamsters could do math," said Jeff, impressed. "Did he get the answers right?"

"Every single one," said Cari. "I wondered how you got so smart all of a sudden."

"I can't spend the entire year trying to keep that hamster quiet!" I moaned.

"He sounds like you," laughed Jeff. "'Cause you're always making comments in class, too."

I looked up at Jeff. "I feel sorry for Mr. D if he goes this crazy trying to shut me up. From now on, I'm going to keep quiet."

"Yeah, right," laughed Jeff. "Good one."

"Meanwhile . . ." said Cari, chewing her thumbnail. "What can we do about Nibbles? Maybe we should kidnap him again and take him to your house for good."

Jeff shook his head. "Nibbles can't keep his mouth shut. He'd talk, and eventually Buzzy's mom or dad would hear him."

"Guys," I said, "there's only one solution. We have to tell Mr. D and the class that Nibbles can talk."

Jeff and Cari stared at me, bug-eyed. "Are you nuts?" Jeff demanded. "We just spent all this time breaking our necks to keep the talking hamster a secret. Now we're going to give up and tell the whole class?"

"What if Nibbles gets taken away?" Cari blurted. "I don't want anything to happen to him. I love that little guy. If it weren't for him, I wouldn't have any friends."

Cari *didn't* have any friends. She'd been hanging around with me and Jeff. But then I realized what she meant and felt my ears get hot. I had to change the subject.

"I know how you feel about Nibbles," I said. "I don't want anything to happen to him either. But if we warn everybody about those risks, I think they'll keep the secret. Anyway, he *is* the class hamster. Mr. D got him for all of us. Doesn't everyone have a right to know he can talk?"

"You have a point," Cari admitted. "Besides, it's getting impossible to keep him quiet. Eventually, Nibbles will talk right in someone's face."

"I like keeping him our little secret," Jeff muttered. "But if kids are going to find out anyway, I guess it would be better to tell them ourselves."

"We'll have to let Nibbles know what we plan to do."

"Right," Cari agreed. "We can sneak up at lunchtime and tell him." She added sadly, "Wow, this is weird. Just like that, we're giving up this huge secret that we've kept so long."

"Yeah, I know what you mean." I nodded.

I let Cari go first back into the classroom. When I followed, Mr. D had moved on to Social Studies. I hung up the hall pass and headed for my seat, stealing a peek into Nibbles' cage. The furry math whiz was now sleeping, probably in a sugar coma. He stayed asleep until lunchtime.

Cari and I gobbled up our lunch. Jeff was still carrying part of his chicken patty sandwich and his cookie as we hurried up the stairs.

Sometimes Mr. D grades papers in the classroom while he eats his standard lunch, a turkey hoagie and iced tea. Today we lucked out. He was nowhere in sight.

Nibbles was still asleep, half burrowed under a mound of wood shavings.

"Nibbles," I whispered. "Wake up."

Nibbles opened one eye. "What's up, pardners?" he asked sleepily.

"We have to tell you something." I opened the cage door, and Nibbles crawled out, little shaving curls stuck to his fur. He sat on the table, paws together, blinking up at us.

"Nibbles," I began, "you know that we've been keeping it a secret that you can talk. Well, now—" I cleared my throat, "Uh, we've decided to tell the truth to the class and Mr. Del Duca."

"What! Did you fall off your horse?" cried Nibbles. "Why would you tell?"

"Mainly because you can't keep quiet,

and they're going to find out anyway."

Nibbles sniffed. "You're not exactly Mr. Quiet yourself."

Before I could protest, Cari interrupted. "Listen, Nibbles, the point is, if the kids are going to find out you can talk, we should tell them first. Make them part of our secret."

"I need to think." Nibbles closed his eyes. "But my brain has shut down. Wait a minute—I know what the problem is." His eyes popped open. "I'm hungry. I need sustenance." He eyed Jeff's cookie. "Hit me up with a piece of that, Jeff."

"I shoulda known he'd work food into this somehow," muttered Jeff. He broke off a chunk and handed it to Nibbles.

"Thanks." Nibbles munched the cookie morsel thoughtfully. "So, when are you going to break the news about my special talent?"

"Hey! I know," burst out Cari. "Buzzy could include Nibbles' secret in his Me Museum!"

"Why should Buzzy get to tell?" demanded Jeff. "Why can't we all do it together?"

"It was Buzzy's mistake that started

Nibbles talking in the first place. Besides, Buzzy needs something exciting for his presentation."

"You're right," I admitted. "I'm desperate, Jeff. This would save my neck. But my parents and Max and my grandma are coming. They'll find out that Nibbles can talk, too."

"I think they can be trusted," Nibbles said solemnly. "I have confidence in your family, Buzzy."

"This could be really great," Cari went on. "Maybe Nibbles can sing a song. Or solve math problems."

Nibbles put his paw over his heart and crooned, *"My heart is aching, my heart is breaking, Can this really be true?"* Then he added, *"Three-fourths of 96 is 72."*

"All right," said Jeff. "You win, Buzzy. But you've got to ask Del Duca to let me come to your presentation."

"Done!"

I had to make a deal with the furry math whiz, too. I bent down until I was nose to nose with him. "My Me Museum presentation is two days away, Nibbles. On Wednesday, you'll get to be a big star in front of the class. But until then, you need to shut your trap. Zip your little lips."

"You got it, Buzzy." Nibbles drew an X on his chest. "Cross my heart."

Cari held up her imaginary microphone. "News flash! Get ready for the most awesome Me Museum ever presented in Filbert Elementary School!"

I could hardly wait to give my presentation. Monday night I shut myself in my room, sat down at my computer, and began to type. "*My name is Buzzy Baxter, and I have a story to tell . . .*" I spent all night typing, typing, typing till I thought my fingers were going to fall off. And I still wasn't finished.

At school the next day—shocker— Nibbles actually managed to keep his mouth shut. In fact, he slept a lot of the time.

Tuesday afternoon, just before school let out, Nibbles whispered, "So, how do I look?" He had brushed all the shavings out of his fur and cleaned his face. He stared at me with his glossy golden eyes.

I smiled and and gave him a thumbs up. "You look awesome, little buddy."

Nibbles twitched, and his fur rippled. "I feel a little dizzy, pardner," he whispered.

"You must be nervous. Drink some water. That'll help." I checked to be sure his water bottle was full. Then I hurried home. Back to my computer for a typing marathon. Late that night, I finally typed the words **"THE END"** and then went to bed, unsure what tomorrow would hold.

CHAPTER 18

DISASTER STRIKES

Next morning, as soon as I arrived in our classroom, Mr. Del Duca said, "You can set up your Me Museum on the display table, Buzzy." He pointed to the tie he was wearing. "I wore my tie with the candy on it in honor of your Me Museum day, because I know you're going to give a sweet report." He gave a drum roll on his desk to emphasize his corny joke.

I carried my bag to the display table and set out my stuff—a stupid lock of baby hair, the robin's egg I found in the backyard, rocks, a picture of me at the zoo in first grade, pictures and seashells from family vacations at the shore, and a baggie of popcorn as a treat for Nibbles after my presentation. My stuff was really boring, especially compared to Lindsey's famous socks and the video Cari had shown featuring herself in one of her mom's TV stories. *Just wait!* I thought and held back a laugh as I recalled the pile of paper that held my autobiography. I was about to spring a huge surprise on Mr. D and the rest of the class.

After ditching the empty bag under my desk, I turned to give last minute instructions to Nibbles. But Lindsey and Amaya were hanging over the science table, playing with him. *Toad turds!* I couldn't talk to him with those two there. I winked at him instead.

From the other side of the aisle, Cari nudged me, "Are you ready?"

I pumped my fist in the air. "I was up half the night typing, but I'm done."

We said the Pledge of Allegiance, and Mr. D took the lunch count. At 9:25, he cheerfully said, "Okay, Buzzy, man your battle station," and I went up to the podium.

Grams, Mom, Dad, and Max arrived right at 9:30.

Dejon, the official greeter, opened the door for them and said, "Welcome to 4-D."

"Hi, Buzzy," Max yelled. "We're here. And so is Scuzzy Bunny to see your Me Museum." She shook her raggedy pink bunny in the air.

The class giggled. Mom shushed Max and waved to me as she squeezed into a small chair. Her shirt looked like she had tucked a basketball underneath. Dad gave me a thumbs-up and Grams blew me a kiss as they sat down.

There was another knock at the door. Jeff stood outside.

"What do you want?" Dejon demanded.

"Hey!" I said. "You're supposed to be the welcome committee, Dejon, not the door police."

Dejon blocked Jeff with his arm. "Welcome to 4-D. Now, what do you want?"

"Mr. Del Duca said I could come for Buzzy's Me Museum."

"That's right, Dejon," said Mr. D. "Lighten up on the defense and welcome our guest. He's practically a member of this class anyway. Jeff, you can sit at Buzzy's desk."

Dejon rolled his eyes and stood aside.

"Hi, Mrs. Baxter, Mr. Baxter," Jeff called as he made his way to my desk.

"Hi, Jeff," Max said loudly. "We're watching Buzzy's Museum."

"Cool," said Jeff. "Me too."

Super Matt was today's announcer. He

walked up front with a grin on his face. "Buzzy Baxter will now present his Me Museum. Get ready to laugh, everybody."

I arranged my autobiography on the podium and cleared my throat. Then I began to read what I'd written over the past two days:

> *My name is Buzzy Baxter, and I have a story to tell about a fourth grade science experiment that led to a crazy result.*

I continued through the first part until I got to "I have a little sister named Max—"

"That's me!" said Max, and a few kids laughed. I glanced around the room impatiently. I couldn't wait to keep reading.

"—and a baby brother on the way . . ." all the way to the part where I talked about Grams staying till the baby comes.

Then I backtracked and talked about when I was born and different parts of my life after that. I held up the shells, rocks, and pictures and talked about them. Pretty lame stuff. Kids were starting to fidget. Dejon stretched his mouth in a yawn, and Mr. Del Duca shot him a stern look. *Don't worry, Mr. D*, I thought. *Wait until I spring my surprise.*

"Basically," I continued, "my life is pretty ordinary. Nothing exciting has ever happened to me. Until last week. The day our class did a science experiment about bursting Bubble Blasts—that's when it happened." I stopped, looking from Mr. D to the class, letting the suspense build.

"What happened?" Amaya asked.

"In my lunch was a thermos containing my grandma's special health juice. I added a couple of drops of the health juice to a little bit of the Bubble Blast mixture, and it fizzed like crazy.

"And then, I accidentally spilled some of the mixture into Nibbles' cage, and Nibbles licked it up."

Jeff leaned forward, waiting. I saw Cari squeeze her hands together.

"Next thing I know, I heard a little voice say, 'Disgusting!' Nibbles was talking! Nibbles, our class hamster, was talking to me."

I had everybody's attention now. Kids stared at me like I was crazy. Some of them twisted around to look over at Nibbles' cage.

"We have a very special hamster in our class. Not only can Nibbles talk, but he loves to sing country music." I told the whole story then—everything that happened from there on. How we were afraid scientists might want to do experiments on him so we sneaked Nibbles out of school and took him home. I told how Nibbles had insisted on the gourmet food from Pet Corral. I included the part where he got lost in the walls and, later, helped save Max. My dad gave me a weird look at that point.

When I got to our run-in with Adrienne Archer, kids nodded and murmured out loud, remembering that whole scene. I repeated how much Nibbles loved food, especially popcorn—which got a laugh—and told how he insisted on shouting out the answers to win candy corn. Reading it out loud brought it all back, how Cari, Jeff, and I worked together to keep Nibbles' talent a secret.

"And now," I concluded, "You are all going to hear Nibbles talk."

CHAPTER 19

THE SOUND OF SILENCE

My heart was pounding as I walked back to the science table, unlatched the cage, and lifted Nibbles out. "Now presenting . . . Nibbles the Talking Hamster! Say something, Nibbles."

Nibbles crouched on my hand, whiskers twitching, bright eyes staring. All eyes—and ears—were glued on the hamster.

I held my breath, waiting for the big performance. But Nibbles just sat there and stared. He didn't utter a word. What was he waiting for? Did he have stage fright?

"Nibbles," I nudged him. "Why don't you sing 'The Star-Spangled Banner'?"

Nothing. Complete silence. What was wrong with the little guy? I remembered what he'd told me yesterday afternoon, about feeling dizzy. Maybe he was sick.

"Say something, Nibbles," I urged softly. "Anything."

A couple of the girls started to giggle. I began to get a sick feeling in *my* stomach.

Dejon slapped his desk. "You are one crazy dude, Buzzy! Only you could cook up a story like this."

"Blaming the hamster for stuff you did," added Matt. "That's brilliant."

"Talk in your hamster voice," Shawnda called out.

Mr. D was giving me an odd look, like, what's Buzzy trying to pull this time?

No one believed me! They thought I was making the whole thing up.

Cari leaned across the aisle. "Nibbles, sing one of your country songs," she pleaded.

"Maybe he needs food," whispered Jeff. "Popcorn. Come on, Nibbles. Sing 'Ramblin' Rose.'" Jeff hurried up front and grabbed the bag of popcorn from my display.

I gave Nibbles a piece of popcorn. He nibbled a tiny bit, but then he just sat there. Why wasn't he chattering and singing and doing math problems?

"He does talk, you know," Jeff told the class angrily. "Buzzy's not making this up."

"Yeah, we heard him too," said Cari. "With our own ears."

"Sure you did!" said Lindsey sarcastically.

"Wow, Buzzy," said Mr. D. "I can't believe you even got Cari and Jeff to back up your crazy story!"

"It's not crazy, it's true!" I yelled.

Everyone was laughing by now—except my parents. Mom had her hand planted on her stomach. Her eyes were wide. Dad looked at Mom like he was asking a question. Mom nodded twice—*yes! yes!*—and Dad stood up so fast, he knocked over his chair.

The baby! My mom was having the baby!

Everyone was looking at my parents now. Dad grabbed Mom's purse and hustled her toward the door.

"I'll stay with Max," Grams called. "We can walk home."

Dad glanced back. "Are you sure you don't want to come? We—"

"Hurry!" Mom held her stomach. She was taking short breaths like she'd just run a race. "I refuse to have this baby in the car!" Mom gasped and grabbed Dad's arm.

Dad's face turned white. "OK, let's get out of here!" he cried.

"Goodbye, Buzzy," Mom called as Dad and Grams helped her out, with Max following close behind. "Your presentation was great!"

The door closed behind them, and a startled silence fell over the room. But soon, the whole class was buzzing. I heard someone say that was the greatest class presentation they'd ever seen. Were they kidding? It was the worst.

"I guess you're about finished, right, Buzzy?" Mr. D asked.

"Yeah," I muttered. I was finished all

right. What a disaster! I put Nibbles back into his cage. He burrowed under the shavings, totally out of sight.

Cari and Jeff moved closer as I laid my autobiography on my desk.

"What do you think happened?" Cari whispered.

"I don't know. Maybe the potion wore off."

"It's okay. We'll give him more of your grandma's health juice," said Jeff.

I put my hands over my eyes. "There is no more. We finished the last batch a few days ago, and Grams can't make any more. She couldn't find the website where she ordered the secret packet of herbs. Maybe it went out of business."

"Oh, man," said Jeff gloomily. "That's major bad news."

"Yup," I said.

Mr. D flicked the light switch to get everyone's attention. "I know you're all wound up. It has been quite a morning. But now it's time to get to work. I'm going to hand out a word search. Find all the words from our spelling chapter, and you get a free homework pass. Jeff, it's time for you to head back to Mrs. Ruiz's room."

Jeff shuffled out the door. As he left, he threw me a long, sad look.

"Lindsey, will you pass out the word search, please?" Mr. D handed Lindsey a stack of papers. "Buzzy, come up to my desk and bring your autobiography along."

Slowly, the class got quiet as kids started working on the word search.

I pulled a chair over to Mr. D's desk and sank into it, excited about the baby coming, but shaky with disappointment. I felt like I'd swallowed a milkshake with hot sauce in it.

"What a morning!" said Mr. D. "Better than a double overtime basketball game!" He tapped the pages of my autobiography. "You did a great job on your presentation, Buzzy. You spoke loudly and clearly. Kept everybody's attention. I should give you a B, because technically, that wasn't an autobiography. After all, most of it was fiction. But your creativity was off the charts! And the way you wove fictional elements about the hamster in with what really happened made the story sound real. Amazing! And the length—I've never had a student write such a long paper." He patted my shoulder. "You've just earned yourself an A+, Buzzy."

"Wow! Thanks, Mr. Del Duca." For sure, A+ was an awesome grade. But that didn't stop the gloom I felt as I walked back to the science table.

"Nibbles." I pressed my face up to the cage. The lump of shavings twitched. Nibbles' face poked out. "Say something," I pleaded. "Come on, Nibbles, did you fall off your horse? You're acting weird."

Nibbles sat on his haunches, his round eyes fixed on me. But he didn't say a word. Nothing. Zipola!

My throat felt raw. Tears stung my eyes. *My heart is aching. My heart is breaking.*

All afternoon I kept waiting to hear that little voice pipe up. *"Surprise! Fooled you that time. Gotcha, didn't I?"* I expected to turn and spot Nibbles rolling on his back, kicking his paws in the air, rocking with laughter. I wouldn't even have been mad at him for making me look like an idiot.

But Nibbles didn't say another word.

CHAPTER 20

INTO THE SUNSET

That night, Grams took me and Max to the hospital to visit my new little brother. Only, my brother turned out to be a sister. Mom had a baby girl!

Rats!

Oh well, Max was happy. Mom too. She had said on the phone that having two boys like me in the house might have been more than she could deal with.

At the hospital we put on plastic visitor bracelets and rode up in the elevator. It was kind of squashy because people's arms were full of flowers and balloons. Max wore her princess gown and carried a bouquet of flowers Grams got for us to give to Mom.

Mom was sitting up in bed. Dad sat beside her on a chair, holding the baby. He peeled back the blanket and said, "What do you think?"

"She's absolutely gorgeous," cooed Grams. "Can I hold her?"

Grams must've needed new glasses. The baby had a squashy little nose. She was tiny and wrinkly and bald as a light bulb.

"She sure is—uh—small," I said as Dad put the baby in Grams' arms.

"What's her name?" demanded Max, whacking Dad with the flowers as she tried to climb onto his lap.

"Teeny Weeny," I said, trying to be funny.

Max giggled at my funny name suggestion. "Or how about Stinky?"

"Or Rose," I said, with a lump in my throat. Nibbles was still on my mind. I remembered his song about Ramblin' Rose.

"Rose . . ." said Mom. "I like that name."

"Rose?" said Dad. "What happened to Sara, like we said all along."

"Look at her," said Mom. "Doesn't she look like a rose?"

"She does have pink cheeks," agreed Dad. "All right. I guess I'm outvoted."

The baby didn't look much like a rose to me. But maybe she'd grow into her name. I raised my eyebrows at Mom. "Remember when you said you wouldn't have the baby on the highway just so I could earn an A on my Me Museum? Well, having her in the middle of my presentation got me an A+!"

"Good for you, Buzzy!" Mom gave me a squeeze.

Mom and Rose came home from the hospital two days later. Grams stayed till the end of the week to help with the baby. Then she had to go home, even though I pleaded with her to stay longer.

"I can't, Buzzy," she said. "I have a yoga class to teach, and my neighbor says Piper isn't eating well. I think that cat misses me."

Dad, Max, and I drove Grams to the airport. When we said goodbye at the security checkpoint, we gave our secret handshake. I hugged her so hard, she said I squeezed the daylights out of her.

"Me too, me too!" cried Max. So we put our arms around Max and made it a group hug.

"I'll miss you, Grams," I whispered. It was hard to imagine her not being at our house anymore.

"We can video chat with each other

at least once a week. Keep me up to date, Buzzy." She gave me one last squeeze.

On the way home, Dad bought us cherry slushes, but that didn't help. I really would miss Grams' pancakes and sense of humor.

In school I had given up expecting Nibbles to talk. He slept a lot and barely moved around when he was awake. It was like he wasn't really there at all. A couple of times, Mr. Del Duca commented on how quiet I was. But the last thing I felt like doing was acting loud and funny.

Friday afternoon, Mr. D told me to hang around after the other kids left.

What was I in trouble for now?

"Buzzy," Mr. D started, "I've noticed you've made an effort not to call out these past few days, and I appreciate it." An odd grin came onto his face. "But the truth is, I miss your funny comments." He held up his hands. "I don't want you to be disruptive or rude, but could you try to find a middle ground? It's kind of boring without your humor to liven up the class."

Was he kidding? Apparently not. He really missed my sense of humor.

"Mr. Del Duca, I'm touched. Okay. I'll

try." We gave each other a high five. "I hope I haven't lost my touch."

"I'm sure you haven't, Buzz. See you Monday."

After school, Cari and Jeff came over. We went in to see Rose, then headed to the kitchen for a snack. I put a box of pretzel rods and a bottle of apple juice on the counter.

"What's the matter?" Jeff asked, digging out a handful of pretzels. "You look grouchy."

"I miss Nibbles."

"Oh. Same here." Jeff crunched the end off a pretzel.

"I wish I'd made him a costume for Halloween," said Cari. "He always wanted to wear sparkly tights." She held up a pretzel rod and spoke into it. "Here at the home of Buzzy Baxter we are dealing with painful news. We will never hear that little hamster sing another cowboy song."

We sat in gloomy silence. The great adventure was over.

Jeff could go only so long before his thoughts returned to food. "Could you hit me up with more apple juice, Buzzy? And how about some ice this time?"

I opened the freezer. As I grabbed a handful of ice cubes, I spotted a small plastic container way in the back, behind a bag of frozen corn. What was that? Wait a minute—could it be? I lifted out the container and read the label.

"Guys," I said in a choked voice. "You'll never guess what I just found!" I turned the container around so they could see the words neatly printed on the label: *Health Juice.*

"Your grandma made that?" Cari asked, wide-eyed.

"Yeah. She must have forgotten about this batch." I started hopping up and down, like popcorn on a hot skillet.

"If we can just remember that science experiment . . ." whispered Cari.

"What was in Mr. D's concoction?" I said. "Baking soda and what else?"

"Vinegar," said Cari. "But wait. Do we really want to do this? If Nibbles starts talking again, we'll have all the same worries we had before—about people doing experiments on him or putting him in a circus."

"Of course we want to do it," cried Jeff. "Weren't we just saying how much we missed the little guy?"

I thought about how much fun it had been having the wise-cracking hamster. Then my brain switched gears to how hard it was to keep Nibbles from getting into trouble. "I don't know."

I looked at the container in my hand. Then I looked at Jeff, who looked at Cari, who looked back at me.

Did we want Nibbles to start talking again?

The answer was as clear as the blue prairie sky.

We got right to work.